ALEX AS WELL

ALYSSA BRUGMAN

Curious
Fox

This novel was submitted as the creative component for a Ph.D. in
Communications at the University of Canberra.

First published in 2013 by The Text Publishing Company, Swann House,
22 William Street, Melbourne, Victoria 3000, Australia.

Published in the United Kingdom in 2014 by Curious Fox, an imprint of
Capstone Global Library Limited, 7 Pilgrim Street, London, EC4V 6LB
– Registered company number: 6695582

www.curious-fox.com

"So What" written by Alecia Moore, Max Martin and Johan Schuster ©
2008, Reproduced by permission of Pink Inside Music Publishing Ltd/
EMI Music Publishing Ltd and MXM Music AB
Administered by Kobalt Music Publishing Ltd

ISBN 978 1 782 02089 9
18 17 16 15 14
10 9 8 7 6 5 4 3 2 1

A CIP catalogue for this book is available from the British Library.
Cover design and typesetting by Jo Hinton-Malivoire
Printed and bound by CPI Group (UK) Ltd, Croydon, CR0 4YY

For Emeritus Professor Belle Alderman AM,
who has taken the most meticulous care of me

THERE ARE MOMENTS in life where something happens and it changes everything forever. You make one decision, and after that you can't go back. It doesn't even have to be a big thing.

Five days ago I stopped taking my medication. I think it might be one of those decisions. How do you know? Maybe if I just start taking it again everything will go back to the way it was? I don't think so.

Five days later I'm in a shopping centre. I'm not going to tell you which one in particular. Just imagine an ordinary shopping centre that stretches out long in both directions, cinched by a four-storey car park.

I slouch into Myer. Unmedicated. I stop in the make-up section, rifling through the nail polishes on special. Alex is with me. The other Alex. I am Alex as well. We are the two Alexes. I guess that's confusing for a lot of people. Sometimes it's confusing for me too.

The girl at the Clinique counter lounges against the display, chewing gum. 'You want a makeover?' she asks. I double-take. Yes, she's talking to me. She's all smooth. Smooth hair, smooth face, smooth clothes. This is what you would look like if you had literally been through the wringer.

'Don't worry, you don't have to buy nothing.' She smiles somewhere behind the mask of her face. I'd like to be all even the way she is.

I hesitate, because five days ago I would have thrust my hands in my pockets and scooted out of there. Instead, I steal across the floor and into the seat she has spun around for me. There's a little mirror on the counter, but it's not facing me. Through it I can see outside the door.

There is a scrolling sign in reverse:

Crockett and Carsell – Conveyancing, Wills, Succession Law

There's pop music playing. It's the Black Eyed Peas. The shoppers are bopping.

'Close your eyes,' she tells me.

The Clinique girl sets to work. She smells sweet and powdery like gardenias and floor polish. She's dabbing things on my face, finger-painting. With my eyes closed I can't tell where she is going to touch next. Her gum-breath blows on my cheeks and neck, giving me goose pimples.

'Cold, lovey?' she asks.

'I haven't had a makeover before,' I confess. I've always wanted to. But I have walked past these counters feeling like a trespasser. As if there was a sign:

PROPER GIRLS ONLY.

But it's more than that. I am all goosepimply and jittery. If I had a tail I would be swishing it.

There's a little tiny brush over my eyelids. I try not to

scrunch them.

'Look up,' she instructs.

She's putting mascara on.

'Can I tidy up your eyebrows a bit?' she asks me.

'Sure,' I say, not realising that she means she wants to tear my hairs out one by one.

My eyes water. I might be crying.

My dad left us last night. I think so, anyway. Last night I kinda thought maybe he just went out, but he didn't come back.

You know how they say to kids, *oh, it's not because of you*. Well, it is one hundred per cent because of me.

'There.' She turns the mirror towards me. 'You're naturally beautiful, but you don't have to be naturally beautiful. That's a lot of pressure. You can even out your skin tones and highlight your best bits. You don't have to go overboard. It's like airbrushing in real life.'

It's not thick make-up like a drag queen, which was what I was expecting. It's not aggressive and dark, like when I do it myself. She's made my eyelids pink and shimmery, and my lips are glossy. I press them together. It feels oily, sticky and tingly.

'It's plumping,' she explains.

You're telling me, says Alex.

I can see his face in the mirror too, a shadow in the background.

He's humming along with will.i.am.

Then the Clinique girl shifts the mirror slightly. There's a guy sitting on one of the couches outside the door. He's about twenty. He looks bored. He's probably waiting for his girlfriend. He's brooding and carefully tousled like the vampire guy. The Clinique girl smiles at me and licks her chops. 'Luscious,' she observes.

'Mmm,' I say, smiling back, pretending to appreciate him too. Alex rolls his eyes.

'You could do something a bit more feminine with your hair. Maybe wear something with a waist. Not that I'm telling you what to do or nothing, it's just that you probably don't realise how pretty you are.'

The Clinique girl lays out the different products she has used on my face on the counter, and I buy the gloss, the mineral powder and the shimmery pink eye shadow. It's expensive, but my parents have always been quite generous with pocket money.

'You have really great bones,' she tells me, handing me my receipt.

One great bone, says Alex.

I snort because it's not a great bone, is it, Alex? No, it's just a teeny, weeny little noodle, you loser.

'Believe in you. Don't be a before picture,' she tells me, as I'm walking away.

'OK,' I say, smiling. 'Thanks.'

I bet she says that to everyone.

In the girls' toilet I braid my fringe across the front the way the girls are all doing it these days. I push my hoodie back and now I am a girlie girl. I stand there looking at my new face. I like this face. It's *my* face. I spend so much time looking at Alex's face – *his* face.

I haven't done this before. I've wanted to since as long as I can remember.

The door opens and my heart beats fast for a second. Sprung. But the woman just walks straight past and into the cubicle behind me. She doesn't even look at me.

Are you OK? I ask Alex.

He shrugs. Wanna buy something with a waist?

We go into the Miss section. A new song starts, Miley this time.

When I walk I swing my hips a little bit. Lazy. Swishing my tail. I run my fingers over the clothing. I slide the plastic coat hangers over the metal racks, digging the screech sound they make. That's the shopping sound.

I find a peasant top that laces up at the front, a halter top, a cute V-necked T-shirt with a butterfly appliquéd on the front and a short skirt. I take them into the changing room. I pull the skirt over my hips, and I try twirling it back and forth in front of the mirror. It's full and short and if I twirl fast enough Alex can see my underwear in the mirror.

I try the halter top on, but I have nothing to fill it. I try the peasant top instead, and I undo the lace,and fluff it out so there is the suggestion that there could be breasts there.

Then I look at Alex and I can tell what he is going to do next.

Don't you dare, I say to him, but he already has his hands down his pants. He is looking at me being a girlie girl in the mirror. He is glaring at the suggestion of where breasts could be. He is imagining big ones. He is staring at shimmery pink eyelids, but mostly it's the lip gloss that does it for him.

I hate it when he does this. It's so gross. It's a real boy thing to do. I say, you are breathing too loud.

He says, shut up.

I say, I found out my dad left this morning. Don't you think it's a little bit insensitive?

He looks at me and sees a hot chick – a smooth Clinique girl. I look at him and see a chimpanzee tugging on his little noodle.

His face has gone red. He says shut up and let me finish. So I pout a little, with the lip gloss on, so he can finish quicker and we can get out of here before the stink of him makes me throw up.

2

WE'RE SITTING IN the foyer of the new school. I am. The other Alex is here too. It's only a few suburbs from the old school, but it feels far enough.

It doesn't matter which school it is. The foyer is like every other school foyer, with those timber honour boards that have gold writing, and a display case full of weird gifts from sister schools in Asia.

On the enrolment form I write: Alexandra Stringfellow, age 14, sex female, religion Catholic.

Is that what you're going to put? Alex asks me.

My pen wavers over the page for a moment.

Shut your face, I say under my breath, because I've decided.

Most of the time I don't need to think about things. I just need to do. Spontaneous. Enrolling in a new school is doing, impulsively. I was literally walking past. They have a big billboard out the front of the school. There's a gorgeous girl looking studious and healthy, and I thought, that's a cool uniform. So I go in there, with my new Clinique ironed-on face, stalk up there and ask for an enrolment form. Just like that.

The rest of the form is supposed to be filled out by my parentslashguardian. My mother is not with me. In any way. I print her name in the space provided. The next question is 'occupation'.

Put 'nutbag'. Alex suggests.

I snigger, because being mental really is a full-time occupation with her.

You know what she said to us this morning? She was writhing about in her bed, weeping, and I put my head around the door to tell her Alex and I were leaving and she said, 'You're killing me, you little pervert. Killing me!'

But that's nothing new. She didn't even say, 'killing us,' like, plural with my dad, because this is all about her.

So this is what we're doing. We're getting a makeover, like a proper girlie girl, and I'm going to a new school.

The rest of the form is about allergies, vaccinations, emergency contact numbers and 'any significant medical conditions'. I leave that bit blank.

You're not going to put anything there? Alex asks me. Nothing worth mentioning?

There's another form where I can pick my electives, so I slip that one to the front.

General wood

Art metal

Music

Building and construction

Drama

Physical activity and sports study

Commerce/law

Automotive

Web design

History

I turn over the page to see if there's anything on the back but that's all there is.

I'm clicking the pen with my thumb. Clickety-click. I probably wouldn't hate commerce/law. I circle that. Maybe history. I could probably google most of the assignments.

We don't need any more drama. Physical activity sounds like lots of getting changed in sweaty change rooms. Nooo, thank you.

What would I pick if I had every subject in the world to choose from?

I would do sewing. But they don't offer it. I know it's a cliché, someone like me being into fashion. I'm not really into fashion, though. I just like girls' clothes. They don't use the same fabrics to make boys' clothes.

Now I am remembering preschool and playing dress-ups with the clothes in the trunk. I have picked a fairy costume. It's just wings and a tulle skirt, but pink. Pinkety-pink. The wings are silky and the skirt is coarse. I liked to rub it between my fingers.

My mother came to pick me up and she looked across the room at me with the pinkety-pink wings on, caressing the tulle skirt. Horror and shame splashed across her face as if I had smeared shit everywhere. That was the first time I understood that there was something wrong with me.

According to her, anyway.

That's how fetishes are born, Alex says solemnly.

No, you were already born with the fetish. Preschool just enabled you, I counter.

He pouts. Alex is kind of set on making it my mother's fault because he doesn't like the idea that it's all my fault.

The only other thing I can remember about preschool is hiding under my bed because I didn't want to go and my dad dragging me out so fast by my ankles that I got carpet burn on my knees.

He was rough with me, Alex says. He would make us wrestle, but sometimes I felt like I was only a tumble away from a hairline fracture.

The woman wants the clipboard back. Her eyes are ice blue. She's pale like us, except it looks better on me.

I quickly circle art metal.

You should have gone for general wood, Alex complains.

You're General Wood, I tell him.

We snigger and the woman looks at me curiously.

The lady from the front office stalks down the hall in front of me. Keys on her hip like a gunslinger. She opens the door to the storeroom and there are school tunics wrapped in plastic bags. It gives me a little shiver. The boys wear black shorts and a grey shirt. The girls' uniform is a red-and-green tartan box-pleat tunic with a belt, and a white shirt with a Peter Pan collar.

I hold it against my body. I am going to wear it with patent leather Mary Jane shoes and knee-high socks. The woman grabs it by the underarms and presses it across my chest, checking the fit.

'Never mind, I was a late bloomer too,' she says.

I can't help but glance down at her big ole baggy boobies, and the distaste must show on my face because she winks at me.

She consults the clipboard again. 'My daughter is in your year. Sierra.'

At first I think she is calling me Sierra. 'Oh,' I say.

Doesn't Sierra mean 'mountain'? Alex asks.

And then there is a silence, so I add, 'I'll be sure to look out for her.'

'I can arrange for her to be assigned as one of your buddies if you like.'

'That would be awesome,' I say.

'That's it then,' she says, shoving my uniform in a plastic bag. 'You just need to bring in a copy of your birth certificate and your immunisation schedule.'

'My what?'

'Your birth certificate, and you should have records of the dates of your jabs. Your mum will know. Are you starting today?' she asks.

'No, I've got a...' I jerk my thumb over my shoulder, as though that will explain. 'A thing...' I finish vaguely. 'A copy of my birth certificate. No problem.'

3

ALEX AND I are waiting in the office of; Succession Law, Crockett and Carsell – Conveyancing, Wills, .Some colour-blind person decorated the place in 1982. It's lemon with a dusty potted plant in a cane stand and a picture on the wall of a person under a palm tree on a beach, except it's all triangles. It looks like a clip art, or an Icehouse album cover.

I am regretting coming here, because if Crockett and Carsell were any good then their office would be flash, wouldn't it?

There is a receptionist behind a wall. She has an opaque glass window between her desk and the waiting room, which she has shut. I guess she sees some unsavoury types.

Like us.

I should stop here, because it's not Alex and me, not really.

We're just the one person. Did you get that already? You guessed it from the blurb, right? I put in some clues.

Alex and I are the one person, but I feel like two people, and this is the problem. It's always been like that, but since I stopped taking my medication five days ago it's so totally clear that I can't be the other Alex anymore. And that's why my dad left us.

Me.

The receptionist slides the window across. 'Mr Crockett will see you now.' She tilts her head towards the narrow, lemon Icehouse hallway.

I tiptoe into the cluttered office. Crockett has hairy eyebrows, and a little snub nose, like a koala. He's probably sixty. He looks over my shoulder for the real client, and when he sees it's only me he looks irritated, and I am embarrassed.

'What can I do for you?' He's bored already, as though this is a prank he doesn't have time for. He thinks I'm going to try to sell him crappy fundraiser chocolate. He's shuffling through papers. He puts one stack of manila folders on top of another stack. He tucks a ballpoint pen behind his ear.

'I need a new birth certificate.'

'You can get that from Births, Deaths and Marriages. You fill out a form. It's quite straightforward. Heidi at reception can help you with that.' He looks at his watch.

I open my mouth but I'm not sure where to begin.

OK, the beginning is this: 'No, I mean a *new* birth certificate. I want to have my gender legally reassigned.'

He stares at me. Then he really stares at me, and he's doing what people have always done as long as I can remember. He's trying to figure out if I am a boy that wants to be a girl, or a girl that wants to be a boy.

I'm staring at him right back because Crockett has hairs growing out of his nose. I don't care how busy or important you are, you can attend to stuff like that.

Why does it matter whether I am a boy or a girl?

But it does. It really, really matters. People want to know which one you are. They want to be able to decide what you are, even when they are just walking past on the street and will never see you again. It's crazy. Most people don't see it as a grey area. They are physically affected when there is confusion.

They are repulsed.

For me it's a very grey area. Greyity-grey. We are the Earl and Countess of Grey, Alex and I.

Now that you know, you're probably wondering what I look like. I kind of have that Tilda Swinton Cate Blanchett Cooper Thompson–ish ice-queen, cleaved-from-stone look. I'm beautiful/ugly. Pale, long and bones. Like a duck carcass. People get an emotional response when they look at me. It's fascination and loathing. Because they can't figure out what I am.

'How old are you?' he asks.

'Sixteen,' I answer, biting my lip. 'Soon,' I clarify.

'In a year … and a half.'

He puts the papers down and folds his hands on the desk. 'I'm sorry. We do wills and contracts, and property title searches. That's our thing here. You are obviously going through something' – Crockett waves his hand, searching – 'profound, but we're not the right fit for you.'

'Where do I go then?' I ask. I pick at my fingernails as I explain. 'I want to go to a new school, but I want to go as a girl, and now they want to see a copy of my birth certificate. It says I am a boy.'

'You could just tell them.'

'Just tell them?'

'Yes.'

I curl my lip. Alex says, 'They're going to go, "Yeah, that's fine, come on in! None of our parents have any problem at all with a transgendered freak getting changed with our little boys and girls. Why, our English Master wears French knickers, and our Scripture Mistress has a very handsome Fu Manchu. You're going to fit right in!"'

Crockett looks at me for a long time. I'm wondering if I've overdone it, and he's pissed. Finally he says, 'Getting your gender reassigned is not something you can undo. Adolescence is a very confusing time. You should probably think about it for a while longer before you make any decisions.'

Now I am pissed, because I wasn't just walking past his shop and thinking, *I know, I might get my gender reassigned today.*

OK, maybe I did, but it's been a long time coming.

You know what it feels like? It's like someone got it wrong to start with. That's what I feel inside. When I was born they went *it's got a noodle, it must be a boy*, but I'm not a boy on the inside.

I say to Crockett, 'Have you ever heard someone sing the wrong lyrics to a song, like that Beatles song, "She's got a chicken to ride"? It's wrong and it seems so silly to you that the other person could think that's how the song goes. But then imagine you heard everyone sing it, like, even the actual Beatles. So you assume that, OK, they must be the real lyrics, even though it's absurd. It's like that.'

The whole time I'm talking, Crockett watches me, but I don't think he gets it. I don't know why I thought he would.

'Have you talked to your parents?' he asks.

My head drops and I stare at my hands. I have painted the nails a dark purple colour, but I bite them and it's half worn off, so it looks more like I slammed my fingers in a door.

'I told my mother,' I say slowly. 'She says I am a pervert and I am killing her.' I pause because the next bit is harder to say out loud, like when you fall off your bike and skid along on your elbows and you're afraid to look because you know there'll be no skin there.

Because at least my mother has the delusion that I can change, that it's some naughty thing I am doing to annoy the crap out of her because I am a teenager and one day I will wake up and I won't feel like I am a girl trapped in a boy's body.

But my dad, he knew it wasn't a joke.

'You should do up your office. It makes you look daggy. It looks like you don't care about your work. Paint it a different colour. And the pictures should be at eye-level because they're for looking at,' I tell him, looking around the room. 'I saw that on one of those renovation shows.'

'What about your father?' he asks.

'I told my dad and he left.'

My lip does this weird, involuntary stretch to the right, so I grab it.

Crockett just looks at me. I don't know what he's thinking. He's all inscrutable, and I am out there on the ledge. I think most people know, just by looking at me, that I have a screw loose, but this is the first time I have opened my mouth and asked for help.

He says, 'I'm sorry.'

www.motherhoodshared.com

This is my first post. Almost fitfeen years ago I had a baby, and after the birth it took them ages to let me hold it, and I was saying, what is it? A boy or a girl? But they just kind of looked at me. They wrapped the baby up, and nobody said anything to me. They were all looking at each other.

So I held teh baby, but I knew there was something wrong.

Finally the paediatrician came in and told me and my husband that our child was, I can't remember the word he used. Sexually ambiguous?

Their advice was to do some tests, and decide which one the baby was more of, and then to raise the child as that sex. But they had to wait until all of my hormones were out of the baby's system. They told me not to breastfeed either. I think I missed out on a special bond there.

The baby had a penis, but not a normal-sized penis. My husband and I thought that if the child has a penis then it must be a boy.

They said the baby also had no testes, but ovaries, and we could have them removed later. He had injections to replace his hormones.

We called the baby Alex – not Alexander or Alexandra, but just Alex.

They wanted to do all this testing all the time, and they got me to keep track of what toys Alex played with and whether he played with girls or boys more, whether he was passive or aggressive. Then when he was four they changed from the injections to oral hormone medication to make sure he kept growing as a boy.

We kept a log, and he went to see a specialist every few months. When you keep a log you can't not think about it. You have to think about it every day. You can't just take your kid to the park and watch them play on the swings. You're constantly analysing and comparing. Every single thing is a sign.

We tried not kkeping a journal for a few months, but the doctors went bananas. They said they couldn't make medical decisions without data and we weren't supporting our son's healthy development.

It's a lot of pressure. My husband and I started fighting, because we always planned to have more children, but then decided we shouldn't in case it happened again. He decided that. I still wanted more kids. Then I went off the pill and didn't tell him, and then later I found out he had a vasectomy and didn't tell me. And, since I'm getting personal here, he did have a scar there and I was worried it was something bad like cancer. It's pretty bad that he let me worry like that.

He thought life was better without the journal. He wanted Alex to stop seeing the doctors. Anyway, long story short, we disagreed about one thing, and then another, and then every single argument we had became a fight about that.

As Alex got older, my husband thought we should explain it to him, but how do you even begin to have a conversation like that with a kid who's already a bit out there? I thought it would be easier for him not to know, and then he wouldn't get anxious about it.

And then last night Alex says to us, sitting there at dinner. I'm a girl. Just like that. Three words.

And my husband explodes at me. I couldn't stop crying. My husband packs up a suitcase and he walks out. He's gone to his borhters place. I'm still crying now.

I can't handle it. I look at Alex and I don't think I love him. I know that if we had a normal child our lives would be so much better.

I want to have a Christmas where I don't go around the shops looking for non-gender specific toys (which are totally impossible to find) and watching his face as his opens the presents for clues as to whether his hormone balance is right. That's not the spirit of Christmas, that's hell.

I am so angry, and I am angry with Alex, and I don't know how to move beyond it. I know that makes me a bad mother. It's also unfair that my husband is rhe one that gets to move out and have a holiday from this life. I am at the end of my tether. I want to have the holiday from my life.

Heather

COMMENTS:

Cheryl wrote:

hang in there, you are in my Prayers daily.

Tammy wrote:

You are lucky to have your kid. The courts are letting my ex manipulate me into custody agreements I feel are unfair. I have visitation now and it's not enough. Be thankful that you have your kid.

Susie wrote:

Please try to not say too much to anyone of a negative nature, and definitely do not share these feelings with anyone. I know it is hard, but once you lose your custodial rights you must almost be Supernanny to regain them.

Jess wrote:

In my opinion hate is an emotion that is needed to heal. But later down the line you may want to try to give that emotion over to God.

Dee Dee wrote:

I hear ya. My twins were C-section and I had blood transfusions. I didn't see them for 12hrs after their birth. I really don't have the same maternal connection with them as I do with my other children.

5

I'M WALKING UP the street towards my house. Alex and I. Is it OK with you if we keep us separate? It makes more sense. We sound like two ordinary kids. Besties, and sometimes we get along great and other times we disagree, just like you and I are friends. Because the alternative is a little bit freaky. I know. It's freaky for me too. I guess we're in this together.

Our house is Tudor-style. And it's always the same temperature. My dad installs air conditioners, so we've got the best available system, usually reserved for maintaining the temperature in commercial wine warehouses, or operating theatres – that kind of thing. Our house is freezing in a constant and predictable way.

It has a turret. It perches on the corner where the two roofs meet. The rest of the house is really badly laid out. Like, the downstairs toilet is next to the fridge, because the kitchen and the bathroom are back-to-back. There's a wall there, but it's still gross. Also, it's three storeys high but the attic is useless. You have to climb up a ladder. And if you want to put anything up there you have to lift it over your head, or hold it while you're climbing the ladder. So basically there is no furniture in the attic. It has a million shoeboxes, which sounds interesting. You could imagine a Shaun Tan book of it, couldn't you? But it's not that interesting. Just documents and journals and old diaries.

Now you go, 'Ooh, old diaries, that could be interesting,' and I thought that too, but they're my mother's and they're full of obscure lists like: Potting mix, light? Anna 10.15. Posted Cindy.

I made that up. It's been a few years since I have looked, and I can't remember *exactly* what they say. The point is that three storeys sounds as though it's grand, but the top floor is a million shoeboxes full of crap. Still, it's totally worth it for the turret, even if you can only see it from the outside.

And there's a lesson in that for all of us, Alex says, doing his best TV evangelist impersonation. I suppose he means that I have an inner turret somewhere compartmentalising all my crap and I'm badly laid out downstairs.

There's no front garden. The house is right on the street. It's on a corner block. There is an oak out the front on the kerb. It looks as if it's been there since the beginning of time. I can imagine it standing there through floods and storms and earthquakes, like a time-lapse movie running in my head. The oak rocks. Some people would look at it and see a thousand coffee tables.

The oak and the turret. Sounds like a pub.

Despite the oak and the turret, which I love, I don't want to go home. My mother is waiting on the front step. She is all bleary-eyed, wearing a rumpled, pilled and wash-faded tracksuit and slippers. She has grey roots. She's been through the metaphorical wringer. She's the anti-Clinique girl.

I stop under the oak, with my hand on its solid trunk. It's letting through a dappled light, and I have this fleeting connection with the planet, as if I am supposed to be here. That doesn't happen very often.

My mother holds her arms out and I sit next to her on the top step while she hugs me and sobs.

Alex is not buying it. My mother is not hugging me to make me feel better, she's hugging me to convince herself that she's not a bad mother, because she can still put her arms around the perverted little freak.

'I love you,' she whispers.

It's the boy Alex being hugged. I stand back with my thumbs in my belt loops.

This hug is all about my mother. It's about her granting the love. It's so generous of her to still be able to love me despite my deformity. I can see her congratulating herself.

She rubs my shoulders. 'Shall we get pizza?'

Because that will make it all better.

However, she is trying. I've been a girl in my head since as long as I can remember, but this is all new to her, so I'm nodding, and we go inside.

I appreciate that this is difficult for her. It's like I'm coming out. Except it's not like coming out, because I'm not gay. Actually, I don't know whether I'm gay, because I find girls attractive, but when I think about sex, which I do a lot (I'm General Wood), it's the girl bits that I find, well, you know. Maybe I am a lesbian. Except that I imagine that I am the girl with the bits.

That's not how other people do sexual fantasies. I don't know how other people do them, but probably not like that. It seems kind of insular, doesn't it? Being both parties? But then since it's all happening in my head, nobody can be offended about not being included, can they? If there's a place you should be able to put yourself first, it's in your own sexual fantasies.

I told you it's confusing. It's easier to think of me as two, isn't it?

The pizza company has one of those automated ordering systems where you have to speak and the computer guesses what you want.

I say 'vegetarian'.

I'm sorry did you say ... librarian? Alex says in his best computer voice. Was that ... agrarian? Did you say ... utilitarian?

I roll my eyes. My mother is standing there and her face is white.

'What about a chicken and bacon deluxe?' she asks.

'I'm a vegetarian,' I say.

I am. I've just decided, right now. Actually, it was when I was under the oak tree, reaffirming my place on Earth. I was thinking about how other people would see that tree as coffee tables, and yet to me it's so much more beautiful being literally a mighty oak.

And then, as if I was hopping across stones in a babbling forest brook, my subconscious went:

I'm

Not

The kind of

Person

Who kills stuff.

And I landed on the other side a veggie.

My mother is screeching. Her face is all purple, her eyes are bulging and there is a vein in her forehead, like the one Julia Roberts gets, but it doesn't make my mother vulnerable and endearing, no, she looks like she's having a forehead hernia. I worry that it is going to burst, and her face will fill with blood under the skin like a big, red balloon which will finally explode and splatter the walls. It's very distracting. I can't understand what she is saying.

I think it went, 'What new cruelty is this?'

Alex calmly holds the phone out to her and says, 'If you want to have a chicken bacon deluxe then have one. No need to have an aneurysm about it.'

I mean, jeez Louise! It's a pizza, woman! Get a grip.

She grabs the phone and starts beating us with it. I shrink away, but she hits me on the shoulder about six times and then she misses me and gets the wall. She takes a breath and has another brain explosion. This time she starts crying and trying to hug me again, but she has boogers, and it's gross. I back away, so the kitchen bench is between us.

My mother screams, 'Why won't you touch me?'

Alex says, 'Because you have halitosis.'

Which is true. My mother has chronic gum disease and it fair knocks me out of the park, and that's why I haven't wanted to hug her for years. I don't even know if I would otherwise, because it has always been that way, and so I'm conditioned to turning my head away from her stinkety-stink breath.

I know it sounds like I am being totally rational through this, but it's shock, and also I'm not shocked at all. I'm kind of used to it, because … my mother has always been …

Imagine if Uluru is absolute serenity and the ocean is homicidally mental, then my mother has been driving up and down the Pacific Highway for as long as I can remember.

Sometimes she might get as far inland as, say, Mudgee, but then she kind of shakes herself out of it and heads back to the coast.

My mother drops on the ground and she's rolling there on the kitchen floor moaning, 'You're killing me.'

So we're back to that again.

Twenty minutes later the pizza guy arrives. I take twenty bucks out of my mother's wallet and pay him. I tear off two wedges for each of us and put them on a plate and we watch *Bargain Hunt*. The vegetarian is really good. It has feta on it. Salty. It's as if nothing bad has happened, except my mother has hiccups. We're good at pretending stuff wasn't said. We do that all the time.

But I'm still a girl.

6

IN THE MORNING Alex puts on the shirt with the Peter Pan collar, the tartan box-pleat tunic and the knee-high socks. I dab on the shimmery pink eye shadow and the lip gloss. I looked up all these do-it-yourself hairstyles on the net. I've pinched my mother's ceramic straightener to make some soft curls. Then when I'm finished General Wood abuses himself again.

OK, here it is: everything you need to know on the noodle front.

It's really small.

Or alternatively, it's really, really big.

Either way, since there will probably only ever be one owner-occupier, if you get my drift, it functions quite economically. Got the picture? I'm not going to mention it again.

Alex and I are nervous and excited about going to the new school. We steal down the stairs smoothing the pleats and tweaking the seams between my fingers. My mother is standing at the window cupping a coffee in her hand.

She glances at me, blanches and then closes her eyes. She is counting to ten. I can tell what's going on in there. If she scrunches her eyes up and wishes, maybe I will disappear.

I oblige, but I have a lump wedged in my throat, bitter and lemony.

Secretly, when I walked down the stairs, I wanted her to think I was pretty. I wanted her to touch my hair, and be proud of me, and wish me good luck today. Because this is the girl I want to be. Not slutty, or dumpy, but feminine and confident. I like this me.

I enjoy being a girl on the train. I flick my hair out of my face and cross my legs. I inspect my nails. Nobody seems to be questioning my gender. One man even says, 'Excuse me, young lady,' as he moves past, which is a total trip. This young guy up the back is checking me out. He slouches and stares. I look demurely into my lap, but when I look back he is still staring. He holds up his phone and I'm pretty sure he is taking a photo of me.

Which reminds me. I pull out my mobile and look at it, just in case. No messages from my dad.

I tap compose and then I sit there for ages. Eventually I type *hey you*, really quick and press send. I dump it in my pocket. It will buzz if he answers.

As I look out the window I can't help thinking about the pizza incident.

What the hell was that?

My mother does try to love me. They both do. Why is it so difficult for them? Am I so unlovable that they have to work that hard? I don't know what it's like to be the child of other parents, but I don't think loving your kid should be such a chore.

No new messages.

You might be wondering about all my friends from my other school. Truth is I'm a loner. I have always been a little bit ashamed, because it's been clear, as long as I can remember, that there is something really wrong with me. Kind of like the seagull with the fishing line wrapped around its leg. You know you can't do anything about it so you try not to look at it.

Also, this very bad thing happened, and I can't go back there.

Very bad.

But I'm not going to tell you any more about that because you're already feeling sorry for me, and I don't want that to tip over into something else ... like irritation. Instead I am going to tell you something good about me.

I can clap really fast.

Imagine the fastest clapping ever: well, I can do that. I can do six or seven claps in a second. I'm like a hummingbird. My hands are a total blur. You're trying it right now, aren't you?

OK, so maybe you can do five claps in one second, but can you do six or seven claps a second every second for a whole minute? No, you can't, because that takes a special aptitude and a dogged commitment to fostering it.

I'm not going to do it right now, because there are other kids who have hopped off the train at the same station, wearing the same uniform as me. I follow them through the big sandstone gates, smiling my head off at the giant girl on the billboard out the front, because she could be me. I could be her.

There are good things about me. There are probably as many goods things as there are bad things. I am pretty as a girl. I'm really tall as a girl. I bet I could arm-wrestle any chick here, and half the guys too.

They're having an assembly. There's a sea of kids sitting in the quad. The seniors are in seats up the back. I stand at the side hugging myself because I'm not really sure where I'm supposed to go. A few kids stare at me, but mostly they don't, because I look normal, and since I'm in uniform, they don't know that I'm new.

Someone touches my elbow. She's my buddy, she tells me. Her name is Amina. She's eye level with me. I'm five nine, so she's really tall for a girl too. She has a deep, melodic voice and a mild accent. She's Somali. She's House Leader and Sports Captain, according to two little pins on the lapel of her blazer. Amina is the most beautiful Earthling there has ever been.

The teacher at the front talks about zone athletics, the library fashion parade, and then makes a long speech about how we're not supposed to bully by Facebook.

After assembly and on the way to class Amina looks through my timetable. She frowns, draws her hair back from her face and tucks it behind her ear.

We stop outside a room. Amina slouches against the wall. She tells me a story, which I can't remember, because I am too busy watching her lips. They are really pink on the inside. Sometimes I get little glimpses of tongue, and when she's finished she shrugs and says, '… And that's the way the cookie is crumbling.'

Isn't that adorable?

She tells me where to meet her at recess.

You can see what's going to happen, can't you? I'm going to fall in love with Amina (who are we kidding? I'm already in love with Amina) and it's going to be really, really complicated and totally unrequited, and I'll probably end up with a broken heart – worse, because Amina won't just reject me, she will be *repulsed* by me. She will tell everybody about my noodle, and then I'll have to top myself in a really brutal man-way.

I can see it too.

Maybe it will end up a different way. Maybe I have happened on the only other one of whatever it is that I am. We will be hooking up and I will discover that she has a noodle.

And we will laugh and laugh!

www.motherhoodshared.com

David is staying at his brother's place for a few more days.

I had a good long look at myself yesterday. When Alex came home I was waiting for him. He had some make-up on, but I let it slide. He does wear make-up sometimes, even as a boy. It's the emu craze.

We had a really nice long hug. You don't get to do that often when you have a teenage child. It was so good, as though we had a real connection for the first time in a long time, and then we came inside and I suggested we get pizza as a treat. I've always been very strict about diet, because as a little one Alex had a lot of problems with his bowels, and we found if we were quite strict on the vegetables he was a lot better in that department.

Anyway, we came inside and he picked up the phone and orderered vegetarian! The few times we have had pizza over the years Alex has always, always ordered chicken and bacon deluxe. He announced it, just like that, that he was vegetarian.

I started to cry because yesterday we had a teenage son who liked chicken and bacon pizza, and today we have a vegetarian corss dresser. I don't know what happened.

I don't care if he wants to be vegetarian. I'm happy to support that, it was just the way he came out and said it without any discussion. He didn't come to me and talk about how he was feeling about being a meat eater and talk it through with me, no, he just made the decision and told me afterwards.

It's the same thing as suddenly deciding on being a girl. I was prepared for that in a way. I have been his whole life, but it still came as a shock to me when it happened. I thought there would be some warning signs and that he would come to us to ask more questions. I have been dreading the questions, but in a way the questions would be better than this.

I feel like an outsider. Alex is becoming this person that I don't know. I always dreamed of having a little girl, and going clothes shopping with her, and this is some creepy perversion of that dream. It's horrifying, and I know I'm not dealing with it well at all.

I'm sorry for him, but I am also angry that he feels like he can't come to me to talk. I have always been there for him. I have been so attentive. I have given up the last fifteen years of my life to be attentive to him.

In the back of my head I wonder if we should have made him a girl to start with. Should we have had whatever surgery was needed to make him a girl in the first place?

Heather

COMMENTS:

Dee Dee wrote:

If you'd made him a girl she would have wanted to be a boy. He's a teenager. This is what they do.

Cheryl wrote:

Oh Heather, you are going though hell, aren't you? We are here for you darlen.

Vic wrote:

Have you ever thought Alex doesn't want to actually be a boy but feels unsafe as a boy, and being a girl would make him feel safer? Could it be he's trying to tell you that something in his environment is threatening for him? Maybe bullying issues at school? Have you talked at all to his teachers? What is his relationship like with his father?

Earthboy wrote:

You should be proud of your son for having a conscience about the planet. Do you know the relative carbon footprints of vegetarians to meat eaters?

Georgeous wrote:

I felt this way for a long time and just thought I was a tomboy. I was really depressed because I was a freak without a name. Someone said I was 'bi-gendered' and it really seemed to be right. I'd rather have a boy's body. I switch back and forth from feeling like I should be a boy one day and feeling like I should be a girl the next. It's like having a dual personality only the other one is a boy. Until I figure out what I am I'm going to keep telling myself that I'm both. Lately I've been pretty down.

8

IN ART METAL I'm drawing a picture of our house. Amina does general wood, so I'm on my own. I told you that we should have done general wood, Alex says.

I have to draw because I haven't got the right shoes on to bang bits of metal with a hammer. I'm supposed to have steel-capped boots in case I go into a frenzy and metal and hammers fly everywhere.

The other students are hitting bits of metal with hammers. A few of them stare at me every now and then. Mostly they ignore me.

You know when you arrive late to a thing, you've missed the instructions, and everybody has already started doing whatever they're doing? They know each other's names. They've already formed little groups. I've always felt like that, but this time it's warranted.

There's music playing. Sometimes everyone hits their hammers in time with the beat. It sounds like Tap Dogs.

The teacher's name is Susannah. She has long blonde hair that falls in ringlets. She has a nose ring. She doesn't wear tie-dye exactly, but she wears clothes in layers with beads hanging off them and she smells like sandalwood. Sounds all arty and casual, right? Sounds like she's got rings on her fingers and bells on her toes and goes tinkling around the classroom sprinkling encouragement like a big nurturing teacher fairy.

You can imagine that Susannah is going to be all supportive and I am going to blossom under her tutelage. I will make an art-metal cage and find my inner spirit, and open the door to the cage and set my soul free. There will be butterflies, or white doves, or attractive people smiling and blowing bubbles, which will catch on the breeze and float away over some green grassy hillside with unicorns grazing on it.

The reason we don't use her surname is because it's Eastern European, so it's about ten syllables entirely composed of consonants. She plays music loud because that way we don't talk and we concentrate on our work instead. Susannah is actually an art-metal dictator.

At the beginning of class this guy threw his hammer in the air and caught it. Susannah dragged him over to the seat next to me by the ear. I'm pretty sure that's illegal. He has to draw too.

I am nonchalantly drawing my house and the guy next to me kicks my leg. He has one of those pencil cases where you can slip the letters in that spell your name and his says 'Ty'. That's it. Two letters. He does a chopping action across his throat.

'What?' I mime.

He draws a square on the table and then he rubs it out

with his thumb.

Ty glances furtively around. 'Is this your house?' he asks.

'Yeah,' I answer.

'Can't you do a different one? Something simple,' he tells me.

I look around at other kids banging and crashing with Beyoncé.

I turn the page over and chew on the end of my pencil.

Susannah jingles up and leans over our desk. She picks up Ty's drawing and harrumphs. She drops it and picks up mine. She chuckles.

'What?' I ask.

'You are going to make this,' she tells me. She outlines how I am going to make an exact replica of our house and then put a hinge on the roof to make it a letter box. 'This part will be tricky,' she says, pointing at the page.

I shake my fist. '*Damn you, turret!*'

Ty laughs. He looks at me and there is genuine appreciation in his face. I think we might be friends, Ty and I. Imagine that.

I went to see a Sidney Nolan exhibition one time, because … It sounds like I am arty and intellectual, but the truth was it was raining, I needed a slash, the art gallery was right there, and the Sidney Nolan paintings were on the way to the loos. It wasn't the Ned Kellys, it was just rocks. Canvas after canvas of red rocks, and I was like 'meh', and then I looked up close at the tiny, little brushstrokes that looked like nothing, but then when I stood back they were rocks. It occurred to me that it would be really hard to do, and then my meh turned to wow.

Ty is looking at me like that.

It takes my breath away, because forever and ever people have looked at me like you'd look at a car crash. You pretend you're not looking, but you can't stop looking, and it's like, 'Oh Jesus!' That's how people look at me.

'You have the most amazing face I've ever seen,' he says. He doesn't see a car crash. He's getting a crush on me.

9

AMINA TAKES ME through the quad to the canteen at recess. When we arrive there is an altercation between two boys.

'What's going on here?' Amina asks.

'Damen pushed in!' exclaims one red-faced, little boy.

'Did not! Morgan held my place when I went for a wazz!' Damen protests.

'Right, Damen, go to the back.' Amina points to the end of the queue.

'But Morgan –' he begins to complain.

Amina interrupts him. 'No brabble!' Brabble! I just love that. 'Morgan is not a bookmark,' she continues. 'If you go to the toilet you forfeit your place in the line. Go.'

'Aw,' Damen whines, but he goes. I stare at Amina. 'Three younger brothers,' she explains. 'You?'

'Only child.'

'How sad for you!' she says, genuinely sympathetic. 'Why is that? Is there something wrong with your mother?'

'So many things, it's hard to know where to begin.'

Amina nods solemnly. Beautiful, but not much of a sense of humour.

I buy a bag of soy crisps and a juice and we head back across the playground.

Amina's friends meet at a bench under a big fig tree. There is a girl called Julia, except she pronounces it 'Whoolia'. She is an exchange student from Brazil. And Sierra. The mountain. She has green eyes like a cat. I am with the exotic chicks, so I guess I'm in the right place.

Sierra bumps me with her elbow. 'My mum wanted to make sure we were buddies.'

'The lady in the front office,' I clarify, and Sierra nods.

They ask me where I am from and what school I used to go to, and I wish I had thought about what I was going to say, because I don't know how much to lie.

I tell them we just moved here from South Australia. Then I remember I told Ty that my house was the only house I've ever lived in, and I blush.

What are the chances of these girls talking to Ty about what houses I have ever lived in, really? Zero! Or maybe zero point zero, zero, zero one per cent. I hope.

I change the subject and ask Sierra what it's like to have her mum at school.

'It's OK, I s'pose.' She pulls a face. 'She knows every single thing that is happening in my life every single second. She kind of stalks me.'

I ask Julia about Brazil and about her host family. She shrugs and answers, but then she asks about me again. I bite my lip, scuff my feet and mumble, which is what boys do when they don't want to talk about stuff, but it just seems to make girls curiouser. I'm going to go home and write notes, to get it clear in my head, but right now I have to distract them.

You know what I did? I showed them my really fast clapping. At first they all looked at each other. My heart stopped for a moment, while it occurred to me that they must think I am a looney. It was a mistake. Now I will have to enrol again at a whole new school. But then Amina tries it. She's not very good.

Sierra has a go. She's got the action right, you need to do more brushing so that it's all in the elbow instead of the wrist. Now they are all doing it, and then they start laughing.

'Rihanna does it,' Julia says. 'In that film clip. Which one was it?'

Amina laughs so much tears are coming out, and she says, 'Stop it, or I'll pee!'

Even while I was clapping and laughing like I was possessed, I stored that away. Boys don't say that. I know the song she means – 'Please Don't Stop the Music'.

10

ON THE WAY home on the train I send a text to my mother.

I need steel cap boots 4 metalwork tmrw.

I'm not sure exactly how she will interpret this request as a personal attack, but I'm sure she has it in her. I'm so ready to just do my own thing without having to spectate some long opera with the wailing and the flailing. Can I just have new boots, do we think?

I'll pick u up.

But she would mean from Joey's, my old school, where I don't go anymore, which she should know, since she saw me leave in a different uniform this morning, if she was paying attention.

No I will meet you @ bunnings in 15 mins.

She doesn't answer, so I get off the train and walk down to the Bunnings warehouse. There is a bench out the front, between the lawnmowers and the wheelbarrows. I sit there in the afternoon sun with my legs stretched out and close my eyes.

It was a good day. No, an awesome day. A new beginning.

People *liked* me, and I got a sense of how it could have been from the beginning for me if I'd made a stand a long time ago, like when I was two. I'm never going to be happy, but I could get close now, I think. I could be almost normal. I could have a friend.

Of course, what I have is an opportunity to invent not just myself, but my whole circumstance. I rehearse it in my head.

We have a dairy farm in South Australia. My parents are boutique cheesemakers. We're here because they're selling to the fancy restaurants and delis in the city. We're getting our own counter in the food section of DJs.

Yeah, I used to name the cows. Tiffany. Bianca. Simone. I didn't milk them, though. It's all done by machines. No, seriously, we're not, like, farmers scuffing around in gumboots. It's just the same as any business. We have staff to do all that. We live in a normal house. Now. It has a turret, though. Of course I mean a for-real turret! What did you think I meant – a chimney?

I open my eyes and there is a man standing in front of me with paint-splattered tracksuit pants, and stubble, and skewiff hair. He is staring at little rattling packets of bolts or rivets in his hands. He's done well to come out with only a handful. Bunnings is an amusement park for old people.

It takes me a minute to recognise him. It's Crockett. He looks through me, and then frowns. He doesn't remember me, just knows that he has seen my face before, so he's waiting for me to remind him.

I am about to say something, but my mother stalks up. She has her game face on. Joy.

'I rang Joey's today. They said you weren't there.'

'I'm going to a new school now, Mum.'

She pokes me in the chest so hard it hurts. 'You don't get to make these decisions!' she hisses. 'If you have a problem, mister, you come to me, and we'll talk about it. *I* make the decisions around here. Do you understand me?'

I look away. I am embarrassed, but Crockett remembers who I am now.

'Do you understand?' she insists.

'Yes,' I say. I do understand. That doesn't mean I agree. They are totally different things.

Crockett steps forward, hesitates, steps back again.

'Can I help you?' My mother asks sarcastically.

He ignores her. He rattles his little metal hardware thingies. 'For my daughter. Her vertical blinds are sticking. And I'm hoping these will fix it.' He watches me for a moment. 'That thing?' he says to me. 'I looked it up. It's doable.'

Crockett has a daughter.

My mother puts her hands on her hips. 'I beg your pardon?'

Crockett looks at my mother and back at me again.

'You looked it up?' I say.

He nods.

Crockett looked it up. A smile spreads across my face. I put my hand over it. He nods again, but this time it's like a little salute. We're having a moment, Crockett and I.

My mother waits until he is out of earshot.

'What's doable?' she asks.

I'm trying to come up with a passable story.

'What's doable? You answer me, mister!' her voice more shrill.

52

Irritation wells up in my belly. 'Please don't call me mister,' I mumble through gritted teeth.

She blushes, and laughs. She's trying to boss me around, but she's weak and panicky and helpless. And even scared.

'Can we just get some boots? Please?'

I don't want her to be like that. She's no good to me like this. She can be angry, but if she's going to fight me, she's got to be sure in her own self what she's mad about. You know Lois, from *Malcolm in the Middle*? She hollers at her kids all day long, but I would have Lois for a mum any day. She's yelling at those kids because she's a hundred per cent sure they're doing the wrong thing. When my mum yells it could be about anything. Half the time I'm pretty sure it's not even about me.

11

www.motherhoodshared.com

I thought about what Vic said, and I rang Alex's school to ask about whether he was bullied. The lady at reception said that she would get his year advisor to call me back. Then she asked if this is why Alex wasn't at school this week.

He came downstairs this morning in a girl's school uniform. He looked straight at me so defiant, like a challenge. Another mother told me once, 'only engage in the battles you think you can win,' and that was the best advice I ever got when he was small. A lot of problems resolved themselves when he stopped trying to pick fights with me. Well, he still used to challenge me all the time, but I stopped taking the bait.

It also meant that he won a lot of the time, so I suppose it was less about winning battles and came down to the things I could put up with and the things I couldn't.

He went through a phase when he was about three where he would push his high chair around the house, and then climb up, and he could reach just about anything. I had some stamps, because I was into scrapbooking for a little while, but he pulled them down and stamped all over the furniture with ink. He did that twice. I was angry and so I threw away all my stamps and ink. Then I cried, because I had really enjoyed scrapbooking. I didn't get to do it very often – only when Alex was asleep and the house was clean, and all the bills were paid, and the washing finished, which was almost never. I cried because Alex has been so totally demanding, I'm not even allowed to have a hobby that I don't do. I'm not allowed to own something that's just for me.

It's not about the stupid stamps, it's the fact that I am not allowed to define myself as separate from 'cares for Alex', even with something so innocuous as scrapbooking. Does that make sense?

He got a bottle of cough syrup open once, and I was so scared! Nothing was safe from him. So I said 'right, mister! This is how it's going to be,' and I got really tough about the whole scooting the high chair around, and it worked. It also helped that I locked the high chair in the broom cupboard when he wasn't in it. He was safer and we didn't fight about that anymore.

Today I tried that again. He told me he didn't want to go to that school, he wants to go to a different school. I decided that I would be tough. Tough but fair, and just say, 'this is what the rules are'.

But I called him 'mister'. Twice. I didn't mean to, it just slipped out. It hurt him, and on some level I was glad that he was hurt, because I'm hurting. I'm hurting every day, and he doesn't care now any more than he cared that I wasn't allowed to have a hobby. I wanted him to know what that feels like, so maybe he can appreciate what his behaviour is doing to me and stop it.

I don't want to hurt him, but I also don't know how to make him understand. I want him to be a person who cares for other people. I am overwhelmed by the gender thing, but much more than that I want him to grow up as a person who thinks about his actions and doesn't do things that hurt other people. I want him to be happy, but not at the expense of hurting others. I don't know how you make someone care about other people. How do you do that?

Heather

COMMENTS:

Dee Dee wrote:

Everything you did today was right, except the name that you used. Don't beat yourself up. The approach was a really good one. Stick with it! You need to let Alex know that you are the boss. All children need to have boundaries. They can pound on them as much as they like, but they need to know boundaries are there, and they don't budge.

In the future, if you think you are going to say 'mister', why don't you try saying 'sunshine' instead?

Cheryl wrote:

Know that we will always be in your corner. You are not going through this alone. This is a safe place for you where peo[ple care.

Georgeous wrote:

What did the year advisor say?

Vic wrote:

Let's take a step back for a minute. What was the thing Alex did that you thought meant he doesn't care about others? Do you mean wearing the girl's school uniform? Or telling you about being unhappy at the old school? I'm not clear on how that is hurting you. It sounds more like Alex is establishing an identity. That would have taken considerable bravery, I would have thought. Am I missing something?

Dee Dee wrote:

Alex can decide he doesn't like a school, but he still has to go. Imagine if every parent let their kids stay home who 'didn't like it'? The schools would be empty. The home is not a democracy. The adults have to make the decisions.

Georgeous wrote:

I disagree. If he is unhappy and unsafe then he shouldn't have to go. He's not going to learn and prosper in an unhealthy environment.

Dee Dee wrote:

No, he does have to go, it's the law.

Vic wrote:

This is not about the pros and cons of school attendance, it's about Alex.

Cheryl wrote:

No, Vic. This is about Heather, and she's grieving over the loss of her son, so watch your tone, please.

Vic wrote:

OK, noted, but it sounds like Heather is punishing Alex for things she did when she was three years old. And if Alex knew she was a girl when she was three, but was being identified as a boy, then of course that is going to manifest in some unusual behaviour.

I would have thought that the fact that Alex has enough self-awareness to recognise who she truly is, at this tender age, and the boldness to be herself is something to celebrate, not to mourn. I guess it's just me.

12

WE GET HOME from the hardware shop and my dad is home. I don't say anything. He puts his arms around me and he says, 'I've thought about it, and your mum and I have gone around this all wrong. It's *your* body. They're *your* feelings. What we should do here is support you in any way we can, because this must be really tough for you. Adolescence is tough enough. Will you forgive us?'

I nod through tears.

He holds my face in his hands. 'You're a really pretty girl. Do you now that? But that's not important. You're doing something really brave and being true to what's in your heart and I'm proud of you.'

'Thanks, Dad,' I whisper, hardly able to make a sound through the lump in my throat.

We turn and go into the house. Mum has made a vegetarian lasagne. It's not very good. I'm glad, because it doesn't matter. It's not about the lasagne. She's trying and it's so great. It's huge.

'I bought a vegetarian cookbook today,' she says. 'It's

going to take me a while to get used to some of these recipes. Hey, maybe after dinner we could go through them together? Tomorrow night you can help me make something.'

'I'd like that,' I say.

'Tell me about this new school you want to go to?' Dad asks, ripping off a slice of garlic bread.

I tell them about Amina and her friends, and about art metal, how I am going to make a letter box for our house.

They are listening to what I'm saying. I can tell because when I finish a sentence they don't change the subject and talk about the things they were thinking about while I was speaking.

After dinner we sit down in the lounge room. Dad has his feet on the coffee table and Mum has her legs across his lap. I sit cross-legged in the armchair flicking through the recipe book. We watch *The Daily Show*. They don't even flinch at the swear words.

'Have you got homework?' Mum asks.

'I did it on the train.'

'Good thinking,' Dad says. 'Our little guy has really grown up.'

And then we all freeze, but I say, 'It's OK. It's going to take some getting used to. I understand that.'

We all relax, and Dad says, 'Hey, why don't I run down to the shop and buy us all an ice cream?'

So we had ice cream and I went to bed a happy girl knowing it would all be all right. The end.

Actually, that's not how it happened. Could you tell? I'm sure there are families out there that have nights like that.

There must be, but not in my house. Our house has never been like that. My mother has never suggested I help her cook. She has always shooed me out because I'm under her feet. My dad has never gone out to get us ice cream, but I know he likes sweet things because there are always lolly wrappers under the seat in his car.

I imagine Amina's family. All those kids sitting around arguing, laughing, their dad saying something like, 'keep it down to a dull roar'. I see her mother tall and elegant, and dark in one of those bright-coloured African headdresses, handing around plates of couscous and eggplant, with the scent of cumin and paprika.

I expect Sierra's family are probably more subdued. I wonder if they are religious and pray before their meal, holding hands around the table, heads bent.

Julia might even be telling her host family right now about the fast clapping we did at lunchtime. I hope so. The host father would give it a try and she would explain to him about the brushing action.

Ty might be telling his family about a girl he met today.

I hope one of them tells their family about the new girl at school.

This is what really happened.

We get home from the hardware shop and I go upstairs and put some music on in my room. Adam Lambert. It's perfect. I'm going through all the clothes in my wardrobe.

I am throwing out all the stuff that is sporty and boyish. I'm setting aside all the things that I might still be able to wear. There's not much left. Mum has bought every single thing in blue or khaki. I hold up a jacket. It's a light grey linen. I like the material, but I've never worn it. I never found the right occasion.

If I wore it with a wide belt and sewed on big buttons or flowers, or even bedazzled the pockets. Then I am inspired, because I could pretty much bedazzle everything left here. With bright buttons and blanket stitching, and scarves, I could reuse them. I'd like to ask my mum because she is really into craft. I know she knows how to do these things. We could girlify these clothes. We could do it together, but she won't. She'll make it into a drama. I have always wanted to do craft with her, but she would do a total head-exploding nana.

What have I got left? There are the clothes I bought the other day, a few T-shirts, some jeans and some cargo pants. Meanwhile, the unwearable pile is almost as tall as me. I shove the unwearables into some garbage bags. I have decided to chuck them into the back of the cupboard. She will go nuts if I throw them out.

I need money. I need clothes to wear that match how I feel on the inside. It shouldn't be so hard.

My dad is standing in the doorway. He's watching me, with his head slunk down, like an old dog.

'Can I come in for a minute…?' He was going to say 'son', or 'sport', because that's what he calls me, but I am still in my tunic. I have long socks with ribbons on the top and the steel-capped boots on. I love it. It merges the Alexes. But it has made Dad shut down.

I nod.

He sits on the edge of my bed. There's not much room with all the clothes I have piled up there.

While I wait for him to say something I tug the braids out of my hair. I can see him in the mirror. He's crying.

'Can I be totally honest with you?'

I don't answer, because how do you answer something like that? No? Please keep lying?

He talks really quick, like staccato, and I can tell he's been practising, or at least thinking about it. Obsessing. Brooding. 'I think we've handled this wrong. I've always thought we've handled it wrong, but your mother is the one who is here.'

That's a good beginning.

'And you need to give her a break. She tries so hard, and you're making it as difficult for her as you can. That's hurtful, Alex. You block her out. She's only trying to understand. We both are.'

He puts his hands over his face and his shoulders are moving up and down.

I go back to my drawers and pull out some more T-shirts, sorting them into two piles.

No *sorry I ran off and didn't tell you where I was*. No *sorry you must have been worried about me*. No *sorry I didn't respond to your text message*. None of that. He's just as bad as she is.

There is this show on Nickelodeon and it's called *Back to the Barnyard* or *Down the Barnyard* or something, and the main character is a cow, Otis, with huge pink udders, except Otis is a he. Nobody ever explains why he has massive udders hanging between his legs. None of the other animals ever draw attention to them. It's just not a big deal. Otis is cool. It's hijinks galore. He has a crush on the girl cow. She thinks Otis is hot, even though he has udders. I love that show.

Mum shouts up the stairs, 'Dinner!'

I bound past my dad and down two steps at a time. Not because I'm hungry, but because I want to get away from that awkward situation. I'm standing there on the bottom step staring at the feast on the dining table. She's done a roast. She's cooked the vegetables in the meat juices, and drowned the whole lot in meat gravy. I'm not sure how long it takes to cook a roast, but I think it's hours and in all that time it has not crossed her mind that I'm vegetarian.

'What?' she says.

I turn around and run back up the stairs, pushing past my father again.

'What?' she says, getting all shrill. 'What now?'

13

THE ATTIC, AS I've already told you, is a room full of
shoeboxes. I have been up here before. When I was younger
it seemed like a good place to hide and hang out, but it's
hot and stuffy in summer or cold and dusty in winter, and
in between it's plain boring, so I never really bothered with
it. But now those two are stalking around downstairs feeling
sorry for themselves, and I'm tired of watching them.

Alex is sitting cross-legged.

I'm sick of being disappointed by them, I tell him. I don't
think my expectations are that high. I get that they're hurt,
and it's a shock and all of that. I do, but it's just a skirt! What
is the big deal? Isn't this kind of a wild overreaction?

Well, it's not just a skirt, he says, because if it was, then I
wouldn't be so set on wearing it. If it didn't matter, then it
wouldn't matter to us either.

But the point is that I'm not asking them to do anything
different.

Alex grabs one of the shoeboxes. It's a bit dusty and
dog-eared. Stacked neatly inside are a whole bunch of kids'

craft kits — sew-an-owl pillowcase, fold-up origami racing cars, paint-and-play farm animals — all unopened. I vaguely remember getting these for Christmas one year, when I was about eight.

They always got us the weirdest presents, Alex notes.

Do you remember that book *Fun Science Experiments for Boys*? I'm still not sure why possession of a penis was so important for the science.

Alex shrugs. Well, we didn't have much fun after all, so maybe a functioning penis was needed for the fun-ness?

There is a box marked 'daycare' in my mother's handwriting, so I flip it open. There are papers inside.

Alex hugs his legs and rests his chin on his knees. You know what she could have done? She could have made some peas or something in a different bowl. She might as well have brought out a pig on a spit.

It wasn't about the food. It was about respect.

I think that's really at the bottom of the whole thing. Am I wrong? Is it me?

Is it?

Alex and I stare at each other. He has been rubbing his eyes and his mascara is smeared. His hair is all kinky where I braided it.

What could we be doing differently?

TINY TOTS'
Early Development Centre

INCIDENT REPORT

Dear ___Mrs Stringfellow___ ,

This letter is a follow-up to our conversation on ___14 March___ (date). There has been no improvement in ___Alex's___ behaviour.

Sadly, today he/she was ___punching/kicking___ . We must hold ___Alex___ accountable for his/her behaviour.

I will be documenting any further situations where ___Alex___ is using negative ways to express himself/herself.

___Verbal warnings___ are not showing positive results. Please share with us what strategies you have used at home when correcting him/her.

Please give me feedback so we can work through this with ___Alex___ in a way that benefits all the children in my care.

If this behaviour continues I will have to ___terminate care___ .

ROS FLEMING
Centre Director

Dolly Steps 👣 Day Care Centre

Accident Report

DATE: April 20th   TIME: 11.43

Dear Parent,

This is to report that   Alex   got hurt today.

Injury Details: Fighting in the bathroom

Treatment: Band aid to grazed knee

Please sign and return this notice. Thank You.

Parent's Signature   Heather Stringfellow

Caregiver's Signature   Samantha

Helping Hands
Early Learning Centre

....

Dear Parent,

Your child

- [X] Cries excessively
- [ ] Bites others
- [X] Does not socialise with others
- [ ] Is frequently unwell
- [ ] Has frequent loose stools
- [X] Behaves aggressively
- [X] Does not enjoy activities

We feel at this time ___Alex Stringfellow___ is not emotionally ready for the type of daycare that we offer here at Helping Hands. If you agree to continue to pay for the position, we can hold it open for ___6 months___ . You may wish to return then. In the meantime you might want to try hiring a nanny or leaving him with a family member.

Regards,

Frances White
CENTRE MANAGER

You know, being in the attic is like a metaphor for retreating into my head, because it's at the top. And all these little boxes are full of memories. Compartmentalised. If you had to do an essay on us, you could say that.

You were a little shit, Alex sneers.

Me? I was the one crying excessively. You were the one punching everyone.

Alex considers. He scratches his head. Yeah, I remember that. I knew I'd get in trouble, but I felt this enormous sense of relief when I pushed someone over.

I nod. I remember that feeling too. I couldn't help it. It was kind of like sneezing. Alex is right. I didn't care about getting into trouble. The only thing I ever got praised for – being a 'good boy' – didn't ever feel right to me anyway.

They made fun of us, I add.

On the floor below I hear one of them walking along the hall. They knock on my bedroom door. They wait, but after a while they go back downstairs.

I wrap my arms around my torso. My nipples are sore. I put my hand inside my shirt gently. They are poking up like little flesh teepees. They tingle.

You're seriously growing norks, Alex laughs. I guess if you wish hard enough.

And it doesn't cross my mind to make a connection between these little buds of breasts and the medication I'm not taking.

The medication that made me want to punch people. The medication my parents made me take to make me a boy. It doesn't cross my mind till much later.

14

www.motherhoodshared.com

David came back today. He had a heart to heart with Alex. When David came back downstairs he said he'd really given Alex some things to think about.

Alex locked himself upstairs after that. We took that as a good sign. We think he did spend some time processing what David had said. He didn't eat and I do worry about that. He is so skinny.

David and I had a long talk too. David was great. He reminded me that Alex is a challenging kid. He's smart and he has always pushed the boundaries. It's exactly like Dee Dee said. He is a kid who pounds on those boundaries every day. I just have to be consistent and fair.

I think I am consistent most of the time, and I think I am fair. What I have trouble with is holding it together right at the moment when he is doing the boundary-pushing. I tend to flip out and go, 'what the hell is this new thing?'

I'm OK after I have had some time to think through what's

happened, but right in the moment I react badly. I know that. I need to get better at recognising his behaviour for what it is and being calm and sturdy like a wall. A forgiving, loving wall.

David said that Alex is exploring his world. He is exploring his gender. That's a really normal thing to do at this age. He is just doing it in an unexpected way.

We haven't exactly decided what we're going to do yet. One thing we both agree on is that we're going to let Alex know when he hurts us. We're not going to go on about it, but just calmly tell him how his behaviour affects us. If we're open with him, then maybe he can start to be open with us too.

David reminded me that we love Alex. We love him. We're just going through a thing right now.

If anyone out there has been through something liek this with their teen, please let us know what worked for you.

Heather

COMMENTS:

Cheryl wrote:

This is a fantastic post, Heather, it sounds like you are really working this through in exactly the right way. It sounds like you might be seeing the light at the end of the tunnel with this thing. God bless!

Dee Dee wrote:

The best thing I can say is that you and ur husband need to be totally united. You will need to come up with a plan on how you deal with Alex and work together. Kids need to know that the rules are the same. That the answer is going to be the same whether they ask you or David. But like Cheryl said, it really sounds like you're getting a handle on this. In my experience, kids who have been ruling the roost will fight even harder when you're on the right track, but stick to it and he will come around.

Georgeous wrote:

I'm estranged from pretty much all my family. They kept insisting that I go to a counsellor. They thought it was just hormones and I would get over it. It seems harsh, but it's a good thing. They did their best to make me feel bad, and now I am surrounded by people who choose to love me.

Vic wrote:

I'm a bit concerned about the forgiving, loving wall strategy. Alex is clearly identifying as 'she'. You and David are consistently referring to her as 'he'. Is the first part of your plan for openness to ignore that?

Heather wrote:

I'm grateful that you have taken an interest, Vic. Do you have a teenage child?

15

AFTER A FEW days I know my own way around. I have learned my teachers' names. Nothing has been very hard so far, especially now that I can do my homework on the train. Academically, they've put me somewhere in the middle.

I sit next to Amina in most classes. Sierra sits on the other side of Amina every single time, as though it's a rule.

Amina doesn't talk. She does her schoolwork. She puts her hand up to answer questions, but not in a sucking-up way. She likes learning. She doesn't look at me. I can't stop looking at her. I have imprinted her face in my mind. I can see it when I close my eyes. When I am in bed at night I run a little silent movie of her in my head. Amina frowning. Amina smiling. Amina laughing. Amina serious. Amina sipping juice through a straw.

I have to resist the urge to poke her with my pen. I literally have to hold my own hand to stop myself from touching her. I pinched her arm once. She gave me such a look. Mostly perplexed.

Sorry, that was me, says Alex, sheepishly.

Another day I was just sitting there in maths. We were doing algebra, and it was all quiet, and then I yelled out, 'RRROXANNE!' I picked up that particular earworm on the train in the morning.

Me again, Alex confesses.

Turns out, girls don't do that. The teacher held me back afterwards to talk about suitable behaviour. I just stared at my feet and mumbled in the appropriate places. Because, the truth is, I was singing because I am happy.

Imagine that?

Amina waited outside for me, and as we walked down for lunch she asked, 'Can you run?'

Sometimes Amina disappears at lunchtime. The other girls have told me that she runs. Laps, I guess. Something like that. It's been a mystery.

Can we run? Alex asks.

Of course we can run if Amina wants us to run.

'I s'pose.'

'Will you be on my team?' she asks.

Of course we'll be on her team!

'Sure!'

'Good,' she says, smiling.

You probably want to know more about Amina. You want to know what she likes, what music she listens to, what she thinks about things. I've been wondering that too, except I am afraid.

Amina is like a present, with shiny paper, crisp corners and no visible stickytape. I don't want to open it and discover it wasn't what I wanted.

I know that's kind of a boy thing too, isn't it? I should love her however she is, but what if she liked *Big Brother*? What if I find out her favourite song is 'My Heart Will Go On'? We couldn't even be friends after that. I think I'll just look at her from here, thank you.

I sit with Julia in science. She's smart, but I think she struggles with some of the technical stuff. Or maybe she is just bored. Sometimes she files her nails under the desk. When I see her I call out 'Whoolia!' and she calls out 'Lexia!' and we air kiss.

Julia's lips are a dusty pink. I thought it was lipstick, but that's the actual colour they are. She has a little tiny mo. She gets it waxed, I know because one day the hair was gone and her upper lip and the space between her eyebrows was a little bit red.

I wonder if I will need to do that. I can ask Julia. She will take me to the girl place for dealing with unwanted hair.

Julia's beautiful. Curvy. She has thick, unruly hair that's always escaping.

Alex groans. But imagine her when she's thirty with two kids, all hairy and with a huge arse, he says.

You're such a bitch. You're not satisfied with her now because of how she might look in fifteen years?

You were thinking it too.

That's a stupid argument. No one is going to be hot when they are sixty.

Amina will be elegant and regal even when she's sixty.

We're going to marry Amina and live with her forever and ever.

Excuse me, are you saying that your heart will go on?

You bet your arse it will!

Mrs Barksdale puts up a picture of a snail on the electronic whiteboard, and I feel dread. It makes me sweat. We're going to talk about hermaphroditic gastropods. It's in the curriculum – we did it at Joey's. Everyone is going to snigger and yell out about how gross it is. I can just tell, and I will throw up.

'What's wrong with you?' Julia asks.

'I hate snails,' I say.

But it's OK. Mrs Barksdale's taking a different tack. She's talking about hibernation and suspended animation. Phew!

I sit with Sierra in visual art. We're making a hen out of clay. The teacher says my hen isn't very good. Apparently Sierra's is a masterpiece. I don't understand why her hen is better than mine.

This one kid didn't even make a hen, he made the letters to spell out, *squawk!* When the teacher asked what he was doing, he said, 'Subverting the paradigm.'

You could see her frozen with indecision, because she wasn't sure if it was really clever, or if he was taking the piss. She gave him six out of ten, a bet each way, the same mark as me, and I actually made the chook like I was asked.

I think about reminding the art teacher about that gallery that literally exhibited the work of a two-year-old, but I don't think that's going to make her like my hen any better.

'It's stupid and arbitrary,' Sierra whispers to me, but secretly she's pleased. I can tell by the sparkle in her eye and the sly way she smiles at her hen when she thinks I'm not looking.

My hen rocks, so I don't care what the teacher thinks. And I'm subverting the paradigm in ways she can't even imagine.

We are art, says Alex.

Clucking oath!

It's hard to talk much in art metal since I've been allowed to swing a hammer, but Ty is helping me with my letter box. Now that I'm a girl, it's OK to be incompetent with tools.

He likes me. He comes into my space. He shows me how to use the tools and his hands brush against mine. He asks me stupid questions so that we'll keep talking.

He says to me, 'you have a really long neck', and then he blushes and looks away.

I don't really know what to say to that, so I say, 'Yeah, you too,' and then we laugh.

But then five minutes later he starts laughing again, because he's remembered how I said he had a long neck (which he doesn't) and then he can't stop giggling, and then I laugh at him laughing, and he laughs at me laughing at him. Susannah cocks an eyebrow at us, and I suck my cheeks in like a goldfish, trying not to laugh, which sets him off again.

Then he says, 'You could be a supermodel.'

I curl up my lip.

'What, you don't want to be a supermodel?' he asks incredulously.

'What's wrong with being just an ordinary model? Why do they have to be super as well? You can't just be superhumanly tall, and supernaturally thin, you also have to be *super*.' I lift up my leg and punch the air, as if I'm flying.

He considers for a moment. 'You could be, though. If you wanted to.'

Ty's going to hate you, Alex warns me. Ty's going to punch your head in. He will be so filled with disgust and rage it will overcome him. He might even kill you.

But right now Ty's doing the goldfish face and chuckling as if we're six years old.

We're in the playground, in our spot under the tree. Sierra has just proposed that we have a sleepover on the weekend. All of us girls. It's frothing up in my head like a shaken-up soft drink. I've only ever had one sleepover, and that was in primary school with this kid who tried to burn the school down. Not on that night, but still.

A slumber party!

Alex thinks we should put our PJs on under our clothes so we can just strip off the top layer. We'll need to get PJs with puppies on them, or something.

We're negotiating a venue, with my head going froth, froth, because there are probably all these rules and rituals that I don't know about.

Then a teacher I haven't seen before approaches us. Miss Angela, the school librarian. She wears stilettos and a magenta shift dress. She has a smooth Clinique face. She explains that she is organising a fashion show to raise money for the library.

I look out across the quad. Ty sits up near the hall with a group of about five other guys. Now he is standing a little bit away from his group. He has his hands in his pockets, and he's watching me. He's like a German shepherd.

There's a permission slip, because Miss Angela is going

to take us out of the school grounds to the boutique that is sponsoring the show. A real stylist is going to choose outfits for us to wear.

Her name is Lien, and she used to be a model. Miss Angela is obviously very impressed, because she goes all gushy when she talks about her.

There will be a dress rehearsal on the weekend before the show. We will get our hair and make-up done, and there will be a photo shoot for the catalogue. Then there's the show itself, which will be held in the library. They want our parents to come along.

'Cool!' says Sierra, flushing slightly.

'We can only have three from your year level,' Miss Angela says, handing the permission forms to me, Julia and Amina. 'It's to do with the risk assessment.'

But what she means is that Sierra is too short to look good in clothes. Sierra knows it. I've been picked because I'm tall.

You've been picked because you could be a super-model, Alex says.

Sierra glances at me sidelong, all slitty and hateful, as if it's my fault. She could be a bigger person about it, and be happy that her friends have been chosen, but she's jealous.

Amina bites her lip. She thinks this selection process is unjust. She thinks fashion is stupid and arbitrary. She should be fighting for it to be inclusive, but she is looking forward to dressing up.

'Oh, and when you drop this form back at the front office, bring your birth certificate. You haven't completed your enrolment,' Miss Angela adds.

I nod. 'Sorry, I forgot.'

I could nip it in the bud. I could say I'm not interested in participating, and then Amina would say that too. Julia might do the fashion show by herself, but it wouldn't be a schism. We could go to the show and support her. We would make up banners and cheer.

This fashion show thing is a schism, and it is my fault because if I said I didn't want to do it, Amina would too. It *is* stupid and arbitrary.

Alex is looking at me and shaking his head.

What? I challenge him.

This is a bad idea.

I can see where this is going, too. Of course I can, because I am Alex as well. But I want to dress up in gorgeous clothes and strut up and down the runway like they do in the magazines, swishing my tail. I want to dress up with Amina and Julia and giggle and be girlfriends, arm in arm. I want to be beautiful. I want other people to think I am beautiful. I want them all to look at me the way that Ty does.

It makes me more real now that Sierra is jealous of me. Jealousy is a million times more potent than pity.

It's just clothes, I shrug.

But it's not, is it? Fashion makes the rules about what women should look like. If anyone should be against such a narrow definition of what is an acceptable way of being, it should be me.

What do you think they're going to do if … *when* they find out you're a boy? Alex asks. Why are you giving people reasons to hate us?

But I'm not a boy, I counter.
I beg to differ, Alex says.
You just keep on begging, I reply.

16

AT HOME MY mother serves me a tiny individual vegetarian cannelloni for dinner. I inspect it. There is no meat in it. 'Thanks!' I say, smiling at her.

'You eat it all up now,' she says, patting my hand.

She and Dad are having a meat one, but that's OK with me. We sit at the dining table together. The telly is on in the lounge room, and we all look towards it. Dad is being fussy with the condiments, grinding the pepper and sprinkling parmesan. I push the cannelloni around my plate. It's nice, but I'm working my way up to telling them about my day.

'You can use the side of the fork first, and then you should push the fork into it, like this.' My mother demonstrates.

'Huh?'

'You're using your fork like a shovel.' She scoops the air.

'What's the diff?' Alex asks.

'You should hold your fingers softly, and point your index finger. You should –'

I interrupt her. 'Can we just eat? Please?'

'I'm just saying, that's all. The tines of the fork should face down. If I don't tell you these things, then who is going to?'

'There's a fashion parade on at school,' I tell them.

They look at me.

'And I'm going to … umm, be a model,' I say.

'As a girl?' my dad asks, still holding a pinch of parmesan above his plate – frozen in time.

I shrug. 'I haven't seen the clothes yet, but I guess. Since I am enrolled … going there as a girl.'

You need to bring up the thing about the enrolment. About the birth certificate. Alex whispers in my ear. Do it now.

I know, but it has taken all my courage to tell them about the fashion parade. I push the crumpled permission slip across the table. 'One of you will need to sign this,' I say, as if I don't care.

They trade a look. The form is closer to Dad. He picks it up and reads it. 'Dear Parent, please give permission for your son slash daughter to participate in yada, outside school hours, yada, images will remain the property of the boutique, yada, collect your child from the school grounds…' He quotes on one exhaled breath. He pulls a pen out of his breast pocket, ready to sign.

My mother places her fork on the edge of the plate and stares at him. 'Shouldn't we discuss this?'

'What are your objections?' he asks.

She opens her mouth and glances at me. I study my meal.

I am afraid of her the way you would be if you were in the path of a demented grandmother swinging her shopping bag. It's not her power – it's her unpredictability.

'It's just clothes, Heather,' he says softly.

'It's NOT just clothes!' she shrills.

'Honey, there is no one right way to eat cannelloni,' he says.

'Of course there is!' she says, thumping the table. 'How do children learn not to be pigs at the table if their mother doesn't teach them? This is not about now. When he is older he is going to want to know how to eat at the dinner table in polite company. He doesn't understand that now.'

They glare at each other in silence.

'You said we were going to support each other,' she adds.

Without looking at her he signs the form. I slip it back into my pocket.

About the birth certificate, Alex reminds me.

Shut up already. There's always Crockett.

17

www.motherhoodshared.com

I can't tell you how relieved I am! I have made a discovery, and it explainms everything! Ever since he was little, Alex has been on hormone therapy. Well, I was in his room and I found a little stash of his medication in his bedside table drawer. He hasn't been taking them! That's why this has happened. We've been through all of this nightmare for the last few weeks. He just needs to start taking his medication again and things can go back to the way they were.

It really is quite good luck that he has decided to be vegetarian, because I can make him a separate meal and slip his medication in. So much of vegetarian food is just sloppy mushed up stuff anyway. It's not ideal, but hopefully we should see it take effect in the next couple of days.

I understand now why he must have been feeling so crazy and mixed up. Hormones are such powerful things, and being a teenager on top of that. I am sure his moods will stabilise after this.

I can't tell you what a weight this is off my shoulders!

The only thing is that now he's decided he wants to be a model! Yes, a female model! Modelling clothes. It's got to be one of the only careers that requires that you actually are a girl. It's typical. Still I expect he will stop all of this very soon once the medication has kicked in.

Heather

COMMENTS:

Dee Dee wrote:

That explains so much of what you've been going through!

Vic wrote:

Heather, I understand this is a really confusing time for you, but don't you think dosing up your child with testosterone without telling her is wrong? Is it just me? That's wrong, isn't it? Shouldn't you sit down and talk to Alex about what she wants?

Dee Dee wrote:

If my three-year-old twins refuse to eat vegetables, I don't sit down and talk about it, I bribe, cheat, cajole and browbeat until the vegetables get eaten. That's what good parents do. They don't let their kids decide what's good for them. Parents decide what's right. That's what parenting is. That's how you make good, law-abiding adults.

Vic wrote:

Alex isn't three.

Dee Dee wrote:

OK, what if Alex had ADHD and decided to stopped taking his medication? Would you advocate sitting down and talking about it? What if it was cancer? Or diabetes? What if it was schizophrenia? No, you would make sure the kid took his damn pills!

Vic wrote:

Alex doesn't have cancer. She doesn't have a disease, and it's not up to Heather to decide Alex's identity. It's up to Alex, and right now Alex is not being allowed to make an informed decision about her own body and wellbeing. This is really serious. Some of the changes her body is going through during puberty will not be reversible. She will have to live in that body for the rest of her life. I'm sorry, but in my opinion this is abuse.

Cheryl wrote:

I understand you feel very strongly about this Vic, but with respect, you haven't met Alex. It really is up to Heather to decide what's best for him until he turns sixteen.

Vic wrote:

*Her. Alex is a girl.

Heather wrote:

I appreciate your concern, Vic, but the doctors have examined Alex thoroughly all of his life, and they have made a determination that Alex is actually male. It's not a disease, but he does have a medical condition. He just needs hormonal support to help him develop into a male as much as he can.

Vic wrote:

Isn't it time someone told Alex?

18

WE CATCH THE school minibus to the first rehearsal. There are ten of us. Amina, Julia and I are the youngest. There are three girls from Year Ten and four from Year Eleven. Miss Angela is at the front, and another teacher – a balding man that I haven't met before – drives the bus. When we arrive he pulls out a newspaper and tilts the seat back a little more.

Will we go bald? Alex asks. Because Dad is balding and Poppy – our mother's dad – was bald too. I put my hand on the crown of my head. Plenty of hair there now. But. Something else to worry about.

I assumed the shop doing the clothes for the fashion parade would be a normal shop in a mall somewhere, but it's a warehouse with shiny insulation lining the ceiling and spinning whirligigs that chop up the light. There are clothes on wheelie racks lined up higgledy-piggledy everywhere. In the middle there is a stage. I've seen this before in a bridal shop. You stand on the little dais and somebody fixes your hem. It's not a normal shop – they must do mostly online orders.

The stylist arrives and stands in the background while Miss Angela talks to us.

'Let me make this clear,' she begins. 'I don't want you to be sexy. It's not appropriate. When you walk, you need to walk as though you're late for class. There is to be no cleavage, or upper thigh. The principal is coming to the dress rehearsal, and if he doesn't like the tone, then he will cancel the show, and we won't be allowed to do it again. So let's see your walk.'

We line up and walk up and down the shop. 'No, no, no. Less hips,' Miss Angela counsels us. 'More like this,' she says, pointing to me.

'She walks like a guy,' somebody mutters.

In the background, the stylist, Lien, starts putting together outfits.

'This is about making money,' she explains. 'The audience will be given order forms and they can tick off clothes in the sizes they want, and hand them in as they leave. This means we're doing clothes your mother would wear and school prom dresses.'

Then Lien asks us to strip to bras and knickers, and she will hand out the outfits.

The girls look around.

'Well, come on then, get busy. We're all girls here.'

And then they start undressing. Amina is undressing.

She kicks her shoes off. She reaches back to unzip her tunic. She turns to Julia. Julia slides Amina's zip down. Amina slips the material off her shoulder. The tunic crumples to the floor. Even with the shirt on I can see the curve of her buttocks.

One of the Year Eleven girls has enormous breasts in a pink lace balconette bra. Everywhere I look there are breasts and buttocks. I spin around.

Now Amina is coming towards me, in her underwear. She has a hot, smooth, athletic body.

She reaches towards my zip. She has mistaken my turning away as a request for help. She is close enough to me that I can feel her breath on my skin and the warmth from her body.

Alex is shouting in my head. *They're going to see! They're going to see!*

'No!' I shrink back from her.

It's like some hideous porn cliché. It's a nightmare. I squeeze my eyes shut, but I can still smell their perfume, and something else. A girl smell. It goes up my nose and straight to my groin. I cross my hands in front of the noodle.

'What's wrong with you?' Miss Angela asks.

They're going to see! Alex is hysterical. He's sweating. He's going to cry.

Shut up!

'I don't feel well,' I whisper.

I'm so ashamed.

She stares at me, and then she draws me away from the other girls. 'What is it?' she asks.

I swallow. 'I'm not wearing a bra,' I confess. 'I didn't realise we'd have to get changed in front of other people.' I fan my sweaty face. 'I'm sorry, it's just ... I'm embarrassed.'

She scans my eyes and then she sighs. 'OK, I have an idea.'

Miss Angela draws the wheelie clothes racks into a triangle around me. It's like a changing room. 'Better?' she asks.

I nod at her over the coat hangers.

'Anyone else like to make themselves a changing room?' she asks.

Nobody did. Most of them didn't even look up. They were folding their clothes into piles by their feet or on a nearby chair.

Julia looks at Amina and rolls her eyes.

Lien leans towards Miss Angela and murmurs, 'Is this one going to be a problem?'

Miss Angela shrugs.

I pretend I didn't hear.

Lien throws a red tartan suit over the clothes rack at me. 'Here you go, princess.'

The other girls are pulling their outfits on, and finally everyone is dressed again. Think of road kill. Stinking dead carcasses, half mooshed with flies on. There. That's done the trick.

I smooth the front of my skirt. Smooth, smooth, like the Clinique girl. Then I move the rack aside and I stride out in my red tartan suit and my steel-capped boots, and stop, with my hand on my hip.

Lien and Miss Angela exchange a glance. Miss Angela shakes her head.

'What?' I ask.

'Nothing it's just that –'

'You look like the real thing,' Lien finishes.

19

I'M GOING TO see Crockett today. I shave my legs in the shower. I'm not really sure where you're supposed to stop, so I keep going. It takes ages. I'm definitely going to have to find a better way to do this.

I pull on some knee-high socks with my steel-capped boots. I drag out my old grey school shorts and the butterfly T-shirt. I pull my hair up into two cute piggies on the top of my head. I tie a football jersey around my waist by the sleeves.

In the mirror I look like a boy wearing his sister's T-shirt. I put on really thick eyeliner and draw a star on my cheek with a pink texta. Then I draw little geisha lips. It's weird. It's a bit Gaga, and I love it. Gaga has given girls permission to be drag queens.

I wait until I hear the shower start in my parents' en suite and then I run down the stairs. I pinch a twenty from my mother's wallet and leave a note on the kitchen table.

Running late.

Cya. A xx

My mother has left a bracelet on the kitchen bench. It's

silver with shiny, black flowers and a butterfly in diamantes. It's just junk jewellery from Target, but it's eye-catching, and it goes with my shirt. I undo the clasp and slip it around my upper arm. It looks hot. I can do this high-street chic. I'm like Gok.

I catch a bus into the city and check out the food hall where our shop would be if we were dairy farmers from South Australia selling our boutique cheese in the city. Although, no one has asked me about my backstory for ages.

There are so many beautiful clothes. I go into Cue and try on a few dresses. The shop assistant is all excited. She thinks I'm going to buy something. She keeps throwing dresses at me over the changing-room door. But I don't have enough money on me, and when I leave without buying anything she is shitty.

I find a bedazzler for four dollars in one of those junk shops. I can't believe it. Well, it's a copy. It's called a 'Ka-Jinker'. Onomatopoeia. Marketing genius. It comes with little coloured butterflies and glass buttons.

There is a busker doing the statue thing.

There's an income for someone with zero skills, Alex says.

I snigger. Yeah, because he didn't even come up with the idea of being a statue.

Alex and I go into 'lingerie' in DJs. March straight in. It's all coloured bras at the front, and then the big white spinnakers for the grannies at the back.

There's a pale blue bra with little tiny orange flowers. It's delicate and girlie. I get the cup size thing, because it's common knowledge. I guess I'm an A, but there is a number too. I flick through them. They go from ten to eighteen.

We're going to have to try some on.

Yeah, baby! says Alex, rubbing his hands together.

I grab a ten, a twelve and a sixteen.

I crouch down to the undies. There're G-strings at the front, and then hipster knickers at the back of the rack. They're all lace with a little orange ribbon. I slide a pair out from behind the others so I can get a better look.

Woot! Alex loves it.

'Boo!' says a voice behind me.

Startled, I turn around. It's Ty.

I'm holding undies. I try to put them back on the hanger, but I miss and they fall on the floor. I accidentally pull off a G-string, and that hits the floor too, so I drop the bras I'm holding, stand up quickly, and take a big step away from the undies.

'Wow, you look hot!' Ty says. He takes hold of my hand and lifts it up, as if he is asking me to dance.

'Ta,' I say, shaking him off. I hide my Ka-Jinker in its plastic bag behind my back. He's caught me off guard.

I'm having a mild panic attack, wondering if I've missed something. I don't feel right today.

'What are you doing here?' I ask, taking another sidewards step away from the undies.

'Dentist,' he says, pulling a face. He introduces me to his mother. His mother! In the undies section! With the undies I was going to try on splayed across the floor! She's probably forty-something. Voluminous skirt. Flat sandals. No make-up. A spinnaker wearer, for sure.

'So you're Alex.'

'Hi,' I say, blushing as she appraises me. She has a shirt on a hanger. She waves it in a way that indicates that she intends to try it on, and then she wanders off.

I take another step away from the underwear, but Ty's eyes slide back to the rack.

'Do you want to catch a movie or something after?' he asks. 'I'm only going to be an hour or so.'

'I have a thing,' I say, crooking my neck to the side.

'Oh?' His eyes flick towards the knickers on the floor.

I nod, but I don't elaborate.

'What about after the thing?' he asks hopefully.

'Not sure how long it's going to take.'

A shop assistant whizzes up behind me and gathers up the undies that I dropped. I think about stopping her, and then I change my mind. I'll do it another day when I have money.

'I could wait,' he offers.

'I'm fine,' I say.

He's disappointed. 'Maybe another time?'

'Maybe.'

Ty picks up a bra on the closest hanger. He holds it up in front of me, and then he raises his eyebrows. I know that look. It's the noodle-tugging look. It makes me feel yuck.

'Ty, I, umm, I like girls,' I blurt.

Idiot! Alex says. What did you say that for?

Ty laughs. 'No! Are you serious?'

I scuff my foot. I don't know why I said that. I've never been asked out by a boy before and I didn't want to lead him on. I like Ty. He's funny. I hope we can be mates. I guess I hoped that if I took the possibility of us being together out of the equation he might just like me for me.

97

'You *are* serious!' Ty's mouth drops open, and I see the General Wood look cross his face again. He's not deterred. He's picturing me with another girl. If anything I've made it worse because now I am unattainable, and that makes me hotter. I know because that's how I feel about Amina.

'I haven't exactly told anyone at school,' I say, peeking at him from under my eyelashes. 'But I know you like me, and I didn't want you to think… I want us to be friends. And I'm not just saying, "can we be friends". I like you. I actually want to be friends.'

Ty doesn't understand. My words are going into his ears, but he's not listening. And I'm not surprised because they are stupid, empty words. It was a mistake.

He will tell. I won't get to go to the sleepover.

'Can we keep it between us?' I ask.

Ty slides an imaginary zip across his lips.

But he will tell.

Of course he'll tell, Alex snorts at me. He will text one of his mates before you're even out of sight.

'Well, I better go,' I say, fleeing.

As I make my way through the lunch shoppers, I put my hand up to my temple. I'm getting a headache.

Ty took me by surprise, that's all. I was having a day off today. I was having a dress rehearsal at being a girl, and he made me have to think about stuff I didn't expect to have to think about.

But it will be OK. Won't it?

20

I HAVEN'T MADE an appointment, but Crockett agrees to squeeze me in. When I go into his office, the desk is deeper in files. There is now a pile on the floor. There's a dead pot plant on the filing cabinet. His eyebrows look even wilder. There's a ladder in the corner, and the door to his office has been painted in a fresh coat of exactly what it was before. He has paint on his knuckles. He sees me noticing.

'Renovating,' he says, rolling his eyes, or maybe he's looking at the ceiling or at the rooms upstairs. I can't tell.

'I'm glad you came back. It should be fairly straightforward. I will apply to the court to have a new birth certificate issued. The judge may want to talk to you.'

I nod, taking a seat.

'There is law in this area. It has been successful in the past when the judge felt that denying the application would put the applicant's life in danger.'

How could their life be in danger? 'What do you mean?'

He folds his hands. 'When the judge felt the applicant may self-harm,' he clarified. 'The questions from the judge may tend in that direction. You might need to see a psychologist.'

I lean back in my chair. 'You mean I should tell the judge that if I don't get a new birth certificate that says I am a girl I will top myself? Isn't that, like, holding the judge to ransom?'

'Would you?' He tilts his head to the side like a bird. 'Self-harm, I mean?'

'It hasn't even crossed my mind.'

It has, though. Just between you and me. You know that expression, 'dying from embarrassment'? After the thing that happened at the other school, it did cross my mind. I can't even bear to think about it. Think about something else, quick. Think about Amina.

I try smiling, but my lip twitches.

Crockett feels sorry for me. He pretends to be writing notes, but I think he is doodling. 'It's a bit more complicated than that,' he says. 'When I looked it up, I saw there have been several cases where applicants needed to have their new sex on their passports because they were going overseas specifically to have their gender reassigned surgically. Do you think you will be pursuing surgery when you're older?'

I blush, 'I um, don't need to.'

'You what?' He is surprised. 'I'm sorry to pry, but I need to know the particulars.'

'The particulars?'

Crockett is asking about our noodle, Alex explains.

'I have…' I'm struggling. 'Well, I don't have a scrotum. At all. I have… More of… What I mean is, what I refer to as…'

Crockett waits, biting his lip. He is pulling the yicky face.

Weirdly fascinated, the way he would look at road kill.

'And I have started to grow breasts, I think. Since…'

Since you stopped taking the medication, Alex finishes. I go redder, but not because I am embarrassed. We're putting two and two together. I think again about my parents and what they told me.

Because *she* called it my noodle, when I was small. That's her word. They sat me down and said I was a bit different to other boys.

You think? Alex drawls.

But don't worry about it, she said. Everyone has parts that are different. Some people have more hair than others, some people have different-coloured eyes, or harelips, or birthmarks. My noodle was like a birthmark. I have to take the medication because I am a bit different to other boys. Lots of people take pills or tablets for lots of reasons. Daddy takes them for his blood pressure. Most people take some kind of medication, they told me.

I just hadn't joined the dots before. Medication … and … being … a … boy.

I start again. 'Let me just say that I have looked up normal parts, and what I have is a … foot in each camp.'

'Right,' he says, blankly. 'But, where do you…'

'Where do I…' I wait.

He's clicking his pen against his teeth. 'Where do you urinate from, I mean. Because if you wee from an appendage, then you would be male, and if you wee from not your appendage then you would be female, right? I mean, it's kind of, physiologically, kind of…' He trails off again.

I sigh. 'It would probably be easier if I showed you.' I stand up, putting my hand on the fly of my shorts.

'No!' He pushes back from the desk.

'Want me to draw you a picture?' I offer.

'No, please!' His eyes are wide with panic. His cheeks have gone red.

I peel a post-it note from off his desk. 'I'm going to draw you a picture.'

'Alex! Please don't. It's not appropriate.'

'Not appropriate?' I keep talking while I draw. 'It's appropriate, because I've always been told not to talk about it, and that's how things – important things – got missed, like that I am a girl. So it *is* appropriate, Mr Crockett.'

He is holding up a manila folder in front of his face like a shield.

'I know I'm a freak,' I continue. 'That's not what this is about. The reason I am here is not because I *want* to be a girl. I'm here asking for your help because I *am* a girl.' I slap the post-it on the desk.

Crockett holds the picture at arm's length, squinting, his lips turned down. 'And this is to scale, is it?'

I narrow my eyes. 'Are you trying to be funny?'

Crockett freezes. 'No, I... I...' he stammers.

I laugh. 'Anyway, like I said, I don't think I need surgery. I don't think what's there really needs changing. I don't know if it would help my case, but there would probably be medical records or something, because I went to doctors when I was younger. But then there was this one time there were so many people looking, and my mum cracked the shits, and after that I didn't have to have the examinations anymore.'

Crockett is mortified by this whole conversation, but he's doing his best. He clears his throat and writes notes.

While we're going to embarrassing places, 'I can't pay you,' I tell him.

He looks up from his notes to the piles of crap on his desk. 'Can you paint?' he asks.

21

I'M SMILING TO myself on the train. I have a job. I'll be painting Crockett's place for four hours every Saturday afternoon until it's done. It's not glamorous, but it's a job. My first job.

Rrroxanne.

I can't wait to tell the girls. I'm wondering if I should 'fess up and say I'm just painting, or whether I could tell them I am doing work experience at a solicitor's office. Amina would be more impressed by that. She will assume it's because I want to be a lawyer.

But now I'm going home, and I get an unpleasant rumble in my guts because I think my parents know a lot more about me than they've been telling me.

For example, says Alex, if you don't take your medication you'll turn into a girl.

Because that would suggest that 'girl' is the default setting, wouldn't it? I mean, what the hell is going on here?

I shift in my seat. I need to prepare myself to ask them.

What are you going to say? Alex says.

Hey, Mum, am I supposed to be a girl? Did you know that all along? So why are you totally freaking out, now that I want to be a girl? Shouldn't you have been expecting this?

Why are they insisting that I'm a boy? Why can't they just let me be a girl? I don't get it.

There is sweat on my upper lip. My heart is beating too fast. I pull my sleeves over my knuckles and curl my fists into a ball. I'm not sure what is happening to me.

I'm frightened, I tell Alex.

Me too, he says.

It's drizzling a little. I can see my reflection in the window. I'm pretending to look outside, but I'm actually looking at me, and then I blink because I'm not sure at first, but it looks like there is a hair growing from the end of my chin. It's thick and sharp. I slap my hand over it.

Has that been there all day? Longer? Shit, man!

Pull it out, Alex suggests.

But I can't, because what if it doesn't come out? And people will see me tugging on my chin. Dammit!

Calm down.

Calm down? I look like friggin Gandalf!

OK, then keep your hand over your chin all the way home.

My phone trills and I pull it out of my pocket. 'Whoolia!' I say, plastering on a grin, because I heard somewhere that you sound more confident if you smile when you answer the phone.

I'll tell her I'm an intern. That's what I'll say.

I keep my thumb on my beard.

It's not a beard, it's one hair.

It's a goddamn beard!

'S'up?'

'Are you a lesbo?' she asks.

I breathe in sharply. I put my hand over my chest, willing my heart to slow down, but I can still feel it thumping.

Ty.

I can imagine them sitting around in the playground. Ty would have told one of his mates who would have told another one of his mates and soon everyone would have known. I *knew* he would. Why did I tell him?

Because you wanted the attention, Alex says. You're different. You wanted Ty to know you're different. And it's like the canary in the coal mine. If he can care about you anyway, even if you're different, then maybe they can all love you despite the other thing. The ones that matter, anyway.

Amina. Except she won't. Everything is black and white for her. It's like she doesn't even see the Earl and Lady of Grey. Her brain doesn't work that way.

Amina would say it was none of their business. Julia would say, 'I'm going to ask her,' and then she would have pulled out her phone while the others protested.

She would have held it out of Sierra's reach. Sierra would have clawed at her arm, laughing. Amina would have been embarrassed and looked the other way.

'Well, is she?' Sierra asks in the background.

From the seat opposite Alex nods at me. Because it will make me sound more honest, he argues. Because the truth is that I *am* into girls.

'Yes, I am,' I say. 'Is that a problem?'

I'm a lesbo.

There is a pause. 'I guess not,' she says.

When Julia hangs up I sit with my eyes closed waiting for my heart to slow into a steady rhythm. I'm still sweating. I feel like I've had three double-shot espressos.

I've lost Julia. She says she doesn't care but she does. I don't know about the others, but Julia cares big time. She's got the whole Catholic thing going on.

What the hell is this, anyway?

You're having an anxiety attack, Alex says.

Oh, of course. I've had these before. I take deep breaths. In through my nose, out through my mouth. When my heart and my temperature finally come down, I send a text to Ty.

Ur a tool.

Quick as a flash he texts back.

So what? Ur still a rock star.

Which makes me smile. Lyrics from the Pink song. See? Ty doesn't care. We could be friends. We *are* friends. He gets me. Should I write back?

Alex shakes his head slowly. He looks so sad.

Why?

Because Ty's not your friend. You asked him to keep a secret – a big secret – and he let you down. That's not what friends do.

But I knew he wouldn't keep it.

That's not the point. He let you down.

I think for a moment. Who hasn't let me down? Everybody lets you down eventually.

22

AT HOME I don't want to be with *them*. I'm not ready to have that conversation yet. I go straight to my room and, inspired by Ty, put on some Pink. I lie on my bed ka-jinking around the pockets of my jacket. I think about texting Amina, just to find out if we are still friends.

I tap 'compose' about a million times, and then freeze.

What are you going to say? Alex asks.

Not something that could be misunderstood.

My mother knocks at the door at five-minute intervals to tell me my dinner's ready. I have told her I'm not hungry. Finally, I whisk the door open and she takes a step back. She has a plate of French toast smothered in maple syrup and powdered sugar.

She's holding the plate to the side and looking at me in this weird way, as if I am kind of amusing and manageable only from a distance, but close up, a bit bigger than she was expecting and with potential to be dangerous, like a zoo animal.

Pink shouts at her from over my shoulder.

(So what? I'm still a rock star. I got my rock moves. And I don't need you.)

'I said I'm not hungry.'

'Why don't you just try a little bit?' she asks, trying to hand me the plate, but I don't want it.

'I'm fine,' I tell her.

'Take it, or I'm going to drop it,' she says, holding the plate out at arm's length.

'Mum,' I begin.

'Quick, I'm going to let it go.' The plate wavers in the air for a moment, and then she drops it. I watch it as if it's in slow motion. It flips in the air, and lands facedown on the carpet.

'Now look what you've done!' she says, shocked and fretful.

It crosses my mind to say, I told you I didn't want it. But what's the point? Instead, I shut the door.

My mother hammers on it. 'You've hurt my feelings!' she shrieks. 'Alex? I made that special dinner for you, and you've hurt my feelings! And now you can clean up this mess, young...' There is a pause. 'Just clean this mess up!'

I turn the music up. And sing, 'Guess what? I'm having more fun. And now that we're done, I'm gonna show you.'

I heart Pink, I tell Alex, picking up a belt and ka-jinking silver studs along the edges. You know why? I feel like I know her. Don't you feel like you could hang with Pink? She just lays it all out, and she doesn't care what people think.

Alex has his head in his hands.

What? he says.

I dunno, I say. Sometimes I feel like I have no control over anything, you know? Like Julia. I don't know why I care. We're not even that close, but I wanted her to like me. I enjoyed the Whoolia high-five, air-kiss thing. It made me feel like I belonged somewhere.

At last my mother goes away. I open the door a crack. The upturned plate is still there on the carpet.

Are we going to clean it up? I ask.

He shrugs. He is more worried about what will happen when I go to school tomorrow. Maybe they won't even care.

I tap 'compose' again and I write, *hey you,* pressing send quickly before I can change my mind.

Then I stare at the screen for the next ten minutes. OK, two minutes, but it feels like ten minutes.

Nothing.

That was stupid, Alex tells me. Isn't it worse knowing that she doesn't want to speak to you?

Twenty real minutes later Amina still hasn't answered.

I feel awful in my guts, as if I have eaten a bad hotdog. Because we're really alone, Alex and I. At least I used to have my fantasies about Amina to keep me company.

I hold up my ka-jinked jacket against my chest.

Alex snorts. That's so lame. It's pathetic. It's like something a five-year-old would do.

Maybe he's right. You know what it looks like? I say, giggling. It looks exactly like I have attacked my clothes with bedazzler's cheap-arse cousin!

Alex looks away from me. He's embarrassed because he's crying.

23

WE'VE DECIDED THE best thing to do is get to school early, and that way I can sit there with my back against the wall, instead of walking into a situation all exposed.

I stomp all the way to school in my steel-capped boots. My fists are clenched. Because if someone gives me shit I'm going to punch them in the eye.

My arm is really itchy. I pull up my sleeve and there is a red rash there.

When I arrive, Sierra is sitting by herself in the empty quad. She watches me approaching. Her face tells me nothing.

'Are you always this early?' I ask.

'My mum,' she explains. Sierra travels with the lady from the front desk, of course.

I sit on the bench next to her, slipping my bag down between my feet. We are silent for a moment, and then I figure I should just say it.

'So, umm, do you have a problem with me being' – there is only the slightest pause – 'gay?'

'What? No!' Sierra says, blushing. 'No! Not at all. As long

as...' Then she giggles.

'As along as?' I raise an eyebrow.

'Don't worry, I was just teasing.' She waves her hand at me. 'Never mind.'

'What were you going to say?'

As long as you don't hit on me. That's what she was going to say.

'Actually I think you're pretty cute,' Alex says, and he holds Sierra's eye contact for a moment too long.

What the hell are you doing? I ask him.

You don't think it would make her feel good? Thinking someone had a little crush on her? Her name is mountain, for Chrissake! And I watch her. Alex is right. She's embarrassed, but I think she's also flattered.

You could snog her. She's not ugly, Alex says.

I don't want to snog Sierra. We can't have this argument right now.

'It's a bit gross for me,' Sierra confesses, and her nose wrinkles just a little bit. 'No offence. But you're into what you're into, I suppose.'

I nod. Alex runs his eye over her. 'Which part is gross?'

Stop it! I warn him.

What? We can make her say it, Alex grins.

Don't make her say it. What the hell is wrong with you?

'It's OK, I'm not going to umm...' I sigh. 'Well, it's like you're into boys, but you're not into *all* boys. You know?'

Sierra narrows her eyes.

That was the wrong thing. Now she's pissed at me because you've said she's not attractive enough. You should have left it, Alex says.

You were making her uncomfortable, I tell him.

I was making her hot.

We don't want to make Sierra hot.

Why not?

This time I bump her knee with my knee.

'What the hell are you doing?' she asks.

I lean across and put my arm on the wall behind her, so now she's trapped. I lean in and lick her earlobe.

'What the hell, Alex?' She pushes me away. But I can see gooseflesh running up her arms.

I laugh and then I stand up and stretch. I do three cartwheels in a row across the empty playground.

This is the bit I'm not prepared for. You know what it feels like? This is like white-water rafting. If I don't put my oar in at exactly the right moment I'll get smashed on the rocks.

24

www.motherhoodshared.com

Alex is not eating consistently enough for the medication to work, so I have gone back to a strategy I used when he first went to school. We used to rub testosterone lotion onto his skin when he was asleep.

I've been thinking about what Vic has said, and I do agree on some levels that he is right. Alex is of an age now where he should be able to make his own decisions, but this is the thing – he needs to be a stable person first.

At the moment, while he is off his medication, he can't make the right choices. It's like asking a drunk person to research their superannuation. They're not interested in the long term, they're not thinking clearly. Super is actually really important, and the choices you make now can change your life, but you can't get someone to focus when they're drinking.

Alex is just like that, except instead of alcohol it's hormones. We want to get him levelled out first and then we can have a proper conversation. Bascially we're trying to sober him up, if you like.

I do have Alex's best interests at heart.

I'd like to share with you something that happened when he was younger. He was about four. We'd been to see many specialists. They all wanted to see his private parts and usually they were sensitive about that, but we went to see this one specialist. He was an a**hole. We made an appointment and when we came in he had five medical students there, and they all went around saying how glad they were to be involved with a rare case study. One of them actually had a camera.

The specialist propped Alex up on the bed and then he started to use all these medical terms like androgen sensitivity and karyotypes and Goldberg Maxwell syndrome. I knew what some of them were, but he wasn't talking to me.

Anyway after a while he asked Alex to stand up and drop his pants. Alex looked so scared. So I said no.

The specialist was sighing and rolling his eyes and talking to me as if I was the four-year-old. He said that it was important to give the students this opportunity because these cases came along so rarely, and that I was being hysterical.

He was trying to bully me because all these people in the room wanted to gawk at Alex's noodle – for medical reasons, but gawking all the same.

I have said, from that moment on, he shouldn't have to show it to anyone. No one. Not even us. No one had a right to his privacy, and I am proud that I have always stuck to that. From then on when we went to these appointments he hasn't shown his privates to anyone.

Heather

COMMENTS:

Cheryl wrote:

This is the thing, kids don't come with an instruction manual, and yours is even more tricky than most. But at the bottom of it all, if you have love between you then you can't go wrong.

Dee Dee wrote:

Cheryl is right. There's always going to be hard days and hard decisions. Parenthood is a constant test of your metal. It's clear that you love him and you want the best for him. It's hard to know what that is in a situation like this.

Vic wrote:

*mettle

Georgeous wrote:

Goddammit, Vic, why are you so obnoxiouis?

Vic wrote:

*obnoxious

25

AFTER THE DRESS rehearsal, Lien asks me to stay back.

'We'd like to take a couple of shots of you for the promo material,' she tells me.

Lien riffles through the clothes on the rack. She has me in a golden glittery skirt, and a linen shirt. While we're talking she adds a cravat, and a camel-coloured cape-thing. It's not my style, but the soccer mums are going to go nuts for it.

'The boutique is going to pay you for this shoot. They will probably make up some posters, or even a billboard. Are you OK with that?'

'I guess so.'

'This is Givenchy, you know.'

I look down at the clothes. 'Nice fabric,' I say.

Lien is giving me a look, and I know I'm ignorant. I like clothes, but I haven't really paid much attention to labels.

The photographer is draping purple material over the wall behind the hemming dais.

'How long will that take?' Lien asks the hairdresser, who is running her fingers through a handful of blonde extensions.

'It doesn't need to be perfect. We can do it while the make-up is going on,' she replies.

They surround me. The hairdresser is tugging at my hair. The comb slides along my scalp horizontally.

'Do you know about weaves?' she asks me.

'Oh yeah, of course,' I bluff.

The make-up artist starts dotting foundation over my face.

'You should really try to come to these things photo-ready,' she tells me.

'I didn't exactly know I was going to have my photo taken today,' I explain.

'A girl that looks like you? You should always be photo-ready,' adds the hairdresser.

'You need to apply a foundation from your hair line down to your décolletage,' the make-up artist continues.

Your what? Alex asks.

'A little blush and a neutral gloss to your lips. With your colouring you need smoky eyes, but you should use a grey or brown rather than a black.'

'OK,' I say.

'You don't want to look cheap, or angry.'

Lien is sliding shoes onto my feet.

'She has huge feet,' she says. 'What are you, an eight or a nine?'

I don't know what my shoe size is. Not in girl shoes. But the shoes fit, so I don't need to answer.

The photographer has a light monitor, and he's holding it up.

'Close your eyes,' the make-up artist instructs.

I sit there with my eyes closed and I can hear them all moving around me. Someone is stacking bracelets along my arms. They are all touching me on my face and on my head. They're so close I can feel their breath and I feel like a giant doll, but I also feel special.

'Her ears aren't pierced,' someone else murmurs.

Once they are finished they prop me up against the dais. I have no idea what I look like. My head feels heavy and tight from the weaves. My face is tight and heavy too. The photographer, Simon, starts giving me instructions. 'Turn your knees this way', 'soft hands like a ballerina', 'long neck', 'tuck your chin', 'smile as though you have a secret'.

That's not a hard one to do.

He turns to Lien. 'I love her look. It's quite masculine, really. Striking. I'd like to see her in men's clothes.' He goes back to his gear to change lenses.

'Hey! There's a bowler hat back here!' he calls out. 'We could do a whole Charlie Chaplin thing. It would be quirky and fun.'

'Yes!' Lien clasps her hands together. 'Now you've got me thinking!' She flips through the rack and finds me some pinstriped wide-legged pants. The hairdresser has found a pair of braces. She ties my extensions back into a ponytail.

They're all excited.

Simon puts the hat on me. It drops down over my eyes and they all laugh.

He gets ready to take the photo and then the make-up artist calls out, 'Wait!'

She scribbles a little moustache on my lip with a brow pencil.

I tip the hat forward, tuck my thumbs through the braces and pout.

They go nuts for that.

Lien is looking through the pictures on the camera's little screen. 'This is great stuff. Can I have some of those head shots to send out?'

'Sure, I'll email them to you tonight.'

'You're going to be a superstar,' Lien tells me, pinching my cheek.

Then they all pack up. They don't even look at me. They are all talking to each other, discussing the next job, gossiping, so I go behind the rack and change back into my school clothes.

There is a mirror there and I can finally see myself, with long hair cascading over my shoulder. I turn my head to the side. She's done shading with my foundation. She's bronzed me. It's lighter around my eyes, and across my cheekbones, but I'm almost olive. There's a pink blush. The eyes are really dark. She's put false eyelashes on, and drawn on lower lashes, and black tear stains, like a cheetah.

I rub off my moustache with spit and a tissue.

That's better. I look all plasticky like a Barbie doll. I look smooth like a Clinique girl.

I look like a model.

I like it because you can't even see my real face under there. People can look at my face and not see me at all. They will see what they want to see.

Lien peeks around the corner. 'Who's going to pick you up?' she asks.

'I'm going to take a bus,' I say.

'You don't want me to drive you?'

'I'm OK. It's only a few blocks.'

She considers for a minute. 'I'm going to drive you to the bus stop.' She hands me a roll of notes. 'You be careful with that. Pop it in your sock.'

She has an Audi, soft top. It has leather seats that stick to the backs of my legs.

We head out into the traffic.

'You could use these images from today in your portfolio, if you were interested in putting one together.'

Our mother is really going to go for that, Alex says.

'I don't know. I haven't really thought about it.'

'You should think about it. You could make good money. I did at your age. I bought a car before I was even able to drive it. It gives you a head start. Simon is willing to give these photos to you for free.'

'Oh,' I say.

'They're usually very expensive,' she explains.

She's giving me a look as if I should be really grateful. So I say, 'Ta. That would be great.'

We pull up at the bus stop and she parks. 'I'm going to stay here till you're on the bus.' Lien turns to me. 'I could find jobs for you, if you want. People are always looking for girls with a strong work ethic, and you have a very versatile look. Any jobs I get for you would be legit. I won't book anything weird. You need someone looking out for you in this business. How do you get along with your parents?'

'Um, OK, I guess. Not so great, maybe,' I mumble.

Her eyes narrow. 'Open your own bank account,' she

instructs. 'You're going to make a lot of money. It's going to look like easy money, but it's not. Don't let them spend it for you. Even if your relationship is fantastic, big money will be the end of your family. I'm saying it straight. I've been there.'

'Thanks,' I say again. 'And thanks for the lift. That was really nice of you.'

She asks for my mobile number and I give it to her.

I slip around the corner of the bus stop and count the money. I peep out again. She's still there. I wave. She waves back.

Lien has given me a thousand dollars.

Rrrroxxannne!

26

IT'S FRIDAY AFTERNOON and the bus is chockers. There's a lady next to me playing Angry Birds.

The bus lurches around the corner. We're not going the way I expected. I don't want to be going this way. This way will take me too close to my old school. I start chewing my nails.

The bus pulls in and the Angry Birds lady gets up. A boy in a Joey's uniform is waiting. He was in the year above me. His name is Trevor. He stands back for the lady to disembark and then he jumps up the stairs. There are other spare seats. I stare out the window, willing him not to sit next to me, but he sits next to me anyway. I have my elbow on the sill and cup my chin in my hand. It's awkward.

He's looking at me. I can feel his eyes boring into the side of my cheek. Eventually I have to look back.

I give him a half smile and look back out the window.

'I know you,' he says.

'I don't think so,' I say.

'I'm trying to figure out where from. Did we go to

primary together? What's your name?'

'You don't know me,' I say, quickly.

He shakes his head. 'No, you look really familiar — even with all that make-up you have on.'

'I'm a model,' I tell him. 'You've probably seen me on a billboard.'

That's your method of making him less interested? Alex asks.

'Really?' he asks, wide-eyed. 'Which one?'

I shrug. 'Oh, there's a couple.'

'Like what?'

'Let me think what I've done recently. One for an insurance company, and there was one for a handbag. You don't read women's magazines, do you?'

He laughs. 'You must make heaps of money,' he says.

'I bought myself a car,' I boast. 'I'm not old enough to drive it.'

'What did you get?'

I glance past his head. 'An Audi. You know the soft top ones? In silver.'

'Sweet! How much did that set you back?'

I smile enigmatically. I have no idea how much one of those cars would be. I pick a number out of the blue. 'Fifty thousand.'

'That's pretty cheap, isn't it?' he says.

'Yeah, well, I know people,' I say, airily.

The bus is slowing. 'This is my stop,' he says with regret. 'But maybe I could call you sometime and we could catch up. I'd love to see your car.'

'I'm kind of busy with work and everything.'

He throws his bag over his shoulder. 'I guess I'll see you on a billboard then.'

The bus pulls up outside an old people's home and Trevor skips down the steps.

There is a little old man. He's on the footpath with one of those walkers with wheels. He's sitting on the seat, pushing with both feet, scooting along backwards, and every few seconds he looks over his shoulder. His face is distorted into a grimace. He's escaping.

A nurse in a blue uniform comes running out of the gate. She skids to a stop and looks both ways like a cartoon character. She clocks the man and then she's after him. He sees her, and now he's going like the clappers, swinging his legs. Scoot, scoot.

Go little old man! Woot, woot! Alex yells out. People from the opposite side of the aisle are standing to see.

I'm smiling and watching the little old man. I don't see that Trevor is standing right outside the window staring up at me. He's recognised me. His face is purple.

He's pointing at me. 'He's a... He's a...' He is so furious he can't get the words out. Trevor starts hitting the side of the bus as we pull away.

'Faggot!' he shouts. He runs after the bus for a few strides. 'FAGGOT!'

27

AT HOME I lie on the couch and watch TV.

This afternoon doesn't matter, does it? As long as I catch my normal train, I may never see Trevor ever again. Everybody at my old school will now think that I'm a faggot, but they already did, so what's the diff? Right? So why does it make me feel like shit? Why does it make me feel so jittery? Why do I feel like hunkering down?

My mother comes and sits at the end. She lifts up my legs and puts them on her lap. She rubs the bottom of my feet.

'Someone called Crockett rang for you today,' she tells me.

I don't want her to touch me. She has creepy fingers. They trace over my skin like spiders. I resist the urge to shake her off. She's so needy. She's like a dog that wants to be patted all the time. I draw my knees up to my chin. She rests her hand on my calf.

Get off! Get off! Get off!

'What's up?'

'I'm just tired.'

'Anything I can do?'

Ask her, Alex urges. Ask her now.

'About Crockett,' I begin. 'He's a solicitor. I went to see him because…'

She freezes. She's stopped breathing.

'I need a birth certificate,' I say.

Her mouth draws back from her teeth as if she's tasting something bad.

'That says I am a girl,' I finish.

Her hands curl into fists. 'You're just not going to let it go, are you?'

I put my arms around my knees and stare at the television. You know what she could do at a time like this? Take a deep breath. Chill out.

'No, Mum, I'm not going to let it go. This is who I am. Why are you so fixed on me being something else?'

'And you've always felt this way?' she asks me. The tears are welling up in her eyes. Her hand shakes slightly in front of her mouth. A tremor. It's weird, as though she's stifling a yawn. But maybe she is really asking me to tell her how I am feeling. Maybe just for a moment it could not be about her.

I cover my face with my hands. 'Sometimes I don't know what I am. But what I would like to be on the outside – what I want other people to see – is a girl. I'd rather be a strong-looking girl than a, kind of, girlie-looking boy.'

Now she's crying. 'Do they pick on you? For being smaller? Or more feminine? Is that why you left your old school?'

I sit up. 'Of course they did! I'm a freak, Mum.'

'Don't you dare say that! Miss Sunshine,' she hisses.

That's new, Alex notes.

'You're not a freak. You're different. Special.'

Alex pulls a face. 'Schpeshaw.'

She lurches forward. 'Don't you dare!' I think for a moment she's going to hit me, but she doesn't. A tear spills down her cheek.

'We should have just asked you. We should have waited and asked you.' She shakes her head. 'It seems so simple now. I am a bad mother. I am a terrible mother. Why didn't we just ASK you?' Her voice is getting higher and screechier. She wipes her face with her sleeve. 'Why didn't anyone tell us this would happen? Nobody told us. No one said this was an option. We spent all this time trying to guess.'

What the hell is she talking about? Alex asks.

I don't even know. I get off the couch and head up the stairs.

'Why do you *always* walk away from me? It's torture!' she wails. 'Alex? We're talking about something here. Alex! It *hurts* me!'

I turn around and march back down the stairs. I grab my mother's hand and I lead her into the little nook where her computer is. I find the page I am looking for on YouTube and I click play. Then I go back up the stairs, because I don't want to watch it again. Two seconds later I can hear her screaming and crying. She sounds like she's having an asthma attack.

She runs up the stairs and she hammers on my door so hard it makes the books rattle right off the shelf.

You know the dying of embarrassment thing, which happened at my old school, that I was talking about before?

Well, I totally understand why people take huge drugs. Like heroin, or cocaine. I can understand why you would want to be literally out of your own head, because being inside your own head is unbearable. In fact, the reason I haven't taken drugs like that is because I know that it would be so good to be out of my head that I wouldn't be able to stop.

Besides, I don't know where you go to buy them.

I put my headphones on and practise my very fast clapping. I'm totally in the zone.

28

I TURN UP at Crockett's at nine. He is burrowed so deep into his paperwork that I wonder if he slept in it.

'Hey, Alex. Nice to see you,' he says, emerging from over the top. 'Just, um, help yourself.' He waves his pen towards some drop sheets in the corner. Then he frowns and looks at his paperwork again.

There are a few paint cans, a roller and a brush in a tray. A ladder leans against the wall. I start by moving piles of things into the middle of the room, and then I put the sheets over the top.

I have pulled my hair up into a ponytail. The extensions are so heavy, they've given me a massive headache. I had no idea being a girl would be painful.

We don't say anything at all. Every now and then I can hear him scratching away with his pen on a piece of paper – the flourish of his signature. Sometimes he taps on his computer keyboard. Or he grunts, but I don't think he's aware of it.

Once the sheets are spread, I open up the can of paint. It's orange. Not a Moroccan burnt ochre, but bright orange, like a traffic cone.

I look up. Crockett stares back at me, munching on the end of his pen.

'You said it had to be brighter,' he notes.

'I did not! I only said it had to be different.'

'That's not different?' he asks.

'Yeah, I guess,' I say.

'So? Pull your finger out.'

I look back down at the paint. The man has zero taste. 'It will dry darker, you know.'

'Darker schmarker,' he says, diving into the next manila folder.

I pick up the paint tin and the brush and start cutting in the corners. It's soothing, the thud, thud sound the bristles make against the plasterboard. I like the syrupy weight of the paint on the brush. I'm really careful along the cornice. Taking my time. Doing a good job.

Crockett turns on the radio. Jessie J is singing about money.

Crockett shows me how to wrap up the paintbrush in a plastic bag so it doesn't dry out, and then I start with the roller. After three walls it's making my arms sore, but I push through it.

At lunchtime Crockett goes out to get us a Subway. He doesn't turn the computer off, or lock anything up.

He grabs money out of his wallet and walks out.

I look out the door and see him scooting up the street with his hands in his trouser pockets.

I take the opportunity to do the section behind his chair while he's not there, then I go for a stickybeak.

Down the hall there is another office. The sign on the door says *Carsell*. It's locked. At the end of the hall there is a door that goes to a tiny concrete courtyard at the back of the building. There is a parking space and a wonky metal gate that opens onto a laneway.

There is a bathroom, with a toilet and washbasin, and to the side of that, there's a narrow stairway heading to the apartment above the office. My feet clang as I jump up the metal stairs. At the top I peek through the window, but I can't see much. I make a circle in the grime with my sleeve. There are some archive boxes stacked on a grey office desk, and an armchair with a broken back. There's another ladder leaning against the wall. It doesn't look as though anyone lives there.

When Crockett comes back we sit in the armchairs in reception to eat, to avoid the paint fumes.

'Tell me about your daughter,' I ask him between mouthfuls.

'Grown up now. Natalie. She's overseas. She works for a tour company, as a guide. She's coming home soon, she says. That's why I had to fix the blinds.' He points at the ceiling.

'So you just live with your wife then?'

'Mm,' he replies.

We eat in silence for a while.

After a long pause Crockett says, 'My wife had cancer.'

'Oh shit, I'm sorry.'

'She got better,' he adds, quickly. 'But she ... Sally, her name is, decided she wanted to live with someone who was home more, so she moved in with her sister up the coast.'

I take a slurp of my soft drink.

'That was four years ago. We still get together at Christmas time. All of us. The kids come back. I have a son too. He's married now. But...' Crockett wipes the crumbs from his face with the back of his hand. He looks hunted.

'But what?'

'Oh,' he laughs. 'It's been made very clear to me that I'm the bastard.'

'Are you?'

'A bastard?' He rolls his sandwich paper up. 'Maybe.' He rubs his eye sockets with the heels of his hands. 'Maybe I am.'

I want to ask him why he thinks he might be a bastard. I want to know what led up to that, but I don't want to pry. Mind you, he's seen a drawing of my noodle, if we're talking about being intimate.

'Carsell doesn't work weekends?' I ask.

Crockett uses his straw to stab at the ice in his cup. 'Carsell is Sally's name. I haven't changed the business name because it would mean reregistering, and changing the signage, and getting Sally to sign papers that she doesn't want to sign.'

He scratches his head and sighs.

It's a bit awkward. I try to think of something to talk about that's a little less personal.

'Who lives upstairs?' I ask.

'Nobody at the moment. It's empty most of the time, until Natalie comes home. I have been meaning to clean it out and offer it for rent. It seems a waste. It's quite big, really. Three bedrooms. She doesn't need all that space. She could always stay with me when she comes back. But I've been putting it

133

off because I know I'll end up with ratbags up there.'

'You could rent it to me,' I say, grinning.

'How would you pay for it?' he asks, frowning.

I shrug. 'I can do modelling work. That pays really well. Natalie could still stay. We could be roomies.'

I'm just shooting the breeze with Crockett, but I can also imagine it, you know. Natalie could be really fun. When she goes back overseas, Alex and I would be on our own most of the time, but Crockett would be here during the day and on weekends – a kind of uncle looking out for us.

But now he's looking a bit sour and put upon, and I feel bad because I've already asked him to do this legal work for free.

'I'm joking, but I do want to get out as soon as I can. My mother is like –' I shake my head. 'I hate living there. She's constantly offended. It's as if when I speak she is listening out for things to get angry about.'

He nods. 'Sally was like that. When she got cancer we did the big around-the-world trip to see all the things she wanted to see before she died. We got it cheaper through the company Natalie works for, but still, it was our life's savings. And then when she got better she wanted to continue living that way, and I said, "But you're not dying anymore," and she said that I was being insensitive because she was still dying, just more slowly. And then she would accuse me of trying to use this business that we grew together to make a honeypot for a new Mrs Crockett. To which I would respond that I didn't want to work until I was one hundred and seven, and then she would say at least I had the luxury of making long-term plans. Had I forgotten that she had cancer? And so on and so forth. We had that argument once a fortnight for about a year, and then she left.'

'Is that why you are a bastard?' I ask.

He picks Subway from his teeth. 'I guess so.'

We walk back into his office and it looks good. It's not a colour I would pick, but it works in a strange way. I can't tell from his expression if he likes it or not.

I don't know that Crockett does 'like' or 'dislike' – things just are.

It's getting late now. Almost four. It's taken me most of the day.

'You can come back next week and do a second coat if you like,' he says.

'I'll just clean up,' I say.

As I'm washing out the brushes in the concrete bathroom at the back of the building, I wonder if Crockett would ever consider taking me in as a foster kid. He only needs to house me for a few years. I don't even need him to do anything. He could just say, *nice to see you*, exactly the way he did this morning – casual, familiar, warm and non-judgmental – and I would be totally happy.

29

I LEAVE FOR school early. The playground is empty again when I arrive, and it's all grey. Grey concrete, grey besser blocks, grey sky, except for Sierra sitting on a bench, in her red-and-green tunic, like a Christmas ornament.

She's reading. She sits up straighter when she sees me.

'We should stop meeting like this,' I say, grinning.

'What do you mean?' she asks, her face flushing.

'Nothing.'

'I love your hair,' she says. 'It looks awesome.'

She would totally let us do stuff to her, Alex says.

We don't want to do stuff to Sierra.

Aren't you even a little bit curious about what she looks like under that?

No. I'm not at all curious.

Sierra takes a breath and holds it for a moment. She slips the book into her bag. She was going to say something.

'What?'

'I forgive you.' She exhales.

'You forgive me?' Alex laughs. 'Oh good!'

Sierra frowns. 'I forgive you for what you did the other morning.'

'What did I do the other morning?'

'When you licked me.'

'When I licked you?'

'Yes.'

We stare at each other. Alex is smiling. He takes a step forward. 'Would you forgive me if I licked you again?'

Stop it, Alex!

What? Sierra is totally digging it.

There is something wrong with you. You don't even like her.

Alex takes another step towards her. This is what boys do. We try to get girls to show us their bits.

Yes, but just any girl?

Just any girl. They're all the same bits, but slightly different. That's what's so fascinating. I reckon we could get her to...

Shut up.

Sierra looks out across the playground. 'My mother says to remind you that you're still not enrolled properly.'

'Oh yeah, that's right.'

'What school did you go to before?'

I scuff my foot on the concrete. My mind's a blank. I decide to distract her instead.

'I'm sorry I licked you, Sierra. It won't happen again.'

Look at her, she's disappointed.

'Unless,' Alex blurts before I can stop him.

'Unless what?' she asks.

'Do you want me to lick you again?' I am genuinely interested in where he might be going with this. 'Because last week I was – what was the word you used? Icky? No, you said I was a bit gross.'

'You're not gross,' she says.

'Why thank you, that's really sweet.'

Sierra folds her arms. 'I don't like girls.'

'Good!' I say.

Then I walk off. I don't even know where I'm going, but Sierra is watching me. She totally digs us.

Later, in maths, Amina passes me a note from Sierra.

I liked it.

'What did she like?' Amina asks.

Sierra puts her index finger to her lips.

'I licked her,' Alex confesses, grinning.

'You what?' Amina is looking at me with her beautiful brown eyes. She's looking bored. 'I don't understand what that is.'

Sierra giggles into her hand, embarrassed.

Amina shrugs and returns to her algebra.

Sierra raises her eyebrow at me. It's an in-joke, but it's with the wrong girl. And it feels yuck. It feels nasty.

30

AT LUNCHTIME AMINA asks me if I'm ready to run. She's looking straight at me. Interested in me. Smiling. At me.

'Sure,' I say. I'm still not sure what she's on about, but I'm so glad I didn't stuff it forever with the stupid licking thing that I'm pretty much happy to go along with whatever. I suppose it's something to do with her being Sports Captain.

Amina takes me down to the oval at the back of C block. There are about ten other students, all in their sports uniforms. Ty is there. He's stretching. He stops when he sees me.

'I was just thinking about you,' he says. He gives me this look that's so intense it feels like my skin is burning. I wonder if I look at Amina like that.

I smile back at him, not sure what to say. I don't think I want to know what he's been thinking.

We're going to run one hundred metres, just Amina and me. I nod as if I know what all this is about, but the truth is that I always avoided sports days, with all the having to get changed and being wimpy and soft.

I don't have shoes, so I take off my boots to run barefoot.

Ty lines me up next to Amina. She crouches down. I copy what she does. She's looking ahead, lithe, focused, cat-like. A little aths veteran, obviously.

'Go,' he says.

Amina is gone. I can see the muscles in her thighs when her shorts hitch up. She has her arms tight next to her sides. But I catch up with her. I try to make my stride really long. My heels are smashing into the dirt and my chest is on fire, but I am catching her. It feels incredible. I can feel all my muscles, and the wind in my face, and my heart beating, but, at the same time, I can't think of anything except running. I run as fast as I can. Totally in the moment. I can't remember the last time I did that.

We're side by side. She peeks over at me, then she grins and spurts ahead. She's amazing. She doesn't move like normal people. She's an athlete. She's doing something special with her breathing. She's had serious training.

Suddenly she stops. That was a hundred metres. I don't know what a hundred metres is. We walk back. My heart is racing. My limbs are all tingly. I might have a heart attack.

'Fifteen seconds,' Ty says.

Amina nods.

'Is that good?' I ask. My breath is ragged and short like a cat hacking up a fur ball.

She shrugs. 'It's OK, for a girl.'

'Good enough for regionals?' Ty asks Amina.

Amina looks at me for a minute, considering. She has a tiny arc of perspiration under her hairline. 'I'll put you in the relay if you like.' As though she's doing me a favour. 'I can't have you dancing on people's toes who qualified through the carnival. But you should train, and then the other girls will see that you have ability.'

Ty is smiling his head off. 'Girl, you can run!' He high fives me. 'Now you need to learn how to breathe.'

I open my mouth and close it again.

On the way back up to class, Amina is excited. She is talking about the training we will do together and old rivalries she has had on the track since primary school – people I will meet at regionals – but I have to stop her.

'Amina, I would love to train with you, but I can't be in your team.'

'Of course you can! Can't means "won't try", that's what my old coach always said. You're good, you just don't know it. But I knew it when I saw you. You have the build for athletics. You're very strong and lean. It's the best shape.' She takes my forearm between her thumb and index finger. She is grinning at me, thinking that I doubt my ability.

'That's not it. I just…' I trail off.

Her eyes widen. 'You don't want to? Is that what you are saying? You are lazy?'

'No, no, no,' I protest. 'I'm not lazy, I am happy to train with you. I would love that, but I don't want to compete.'

She stops still. 'Why not?'

Yeah, why not? Alex asks.

Because when they find out I used to be a boy there will be trouble.

When they find out?

That's where all this is heading, isn't it? Someone's going to discover it somehow — about the noodle, and it will all turn to shit. But it would be worse if I represented the school at regionals as a girl. Much worse. People won't just freak out. They'll be enraged.

'Because I don't want to.'

Amina wipes her forehead with the back of her hand. Her shoulders slump. I've disappointed her, and it kills me.

'I'm sorry, but I —'

She holds her hand up, silencing me.

'Thanks for letting me know.'

Amina doesn't talk to me after that, and not even as though she's pissed, more like I am simply not worth getting to know.

www.motherhoodshared.com

Every day is like a big whirlpool, and I feel as though I have to swim as fast as I can all day just to stay out of the plug hole. I'm exhausted all the time.

I don't like me. I don't like the person being Alex's mother makes me.

I realise now I've handled everything wrong. I've done it wrong from the beginning. I have stuffed it all up, and it's too late now. I'm a terrible mother. None of it has come naturally to me. I see other families and they seem to drift through the day.

It's the roller coaster I'm not coping with. Every day is a new fresh hell. I would like to get on a plane and go somewhere where there is a sandy beach and drink something out of a coconut. I think I am going to tell David that he needs to deal with it. It's my turn to take some time off. I'm trying hard to think of a reason not to do it, and I can't think of one.

Heather

COMMENTS:

Susie wrote:

You should do it. You can pay for it all up front. You need a break! It's only a week. It's the best thing you can do right now.

Cheryl wrote:

Sometimes the best thing a mother can do for her kids is put herself first.

32

WHEN I GET home the house is dark. Dad is in the study shuffling papers.

'Where's Mum?' I ask.

'She'll be back in a few days,' he tells me.

They have finally carted her off to the funny farm, Alex says, and we are both so relieved.

'Is she in hospital?' I ask.

'What? No, no, no.' Then he laughs. 'No, she's just gone away for a few days.'

'Where?'

He scratches his head and leans back in his office chair. 'Fiji.'

'Fiji?' I think he might be joking. It's hard to tell, but she can't seriously have just decided to pack up and go to Fiji since this morning. Can she?

'Fiji? Like the island?' I clarify.

'Yes.'

We stare at each other.

'Did you know she was going to Fiji?' I ask.

He looks away. 'I had a few days off, so it seems fair that she has a few days off too.'

'When do I get to have a few days off?' I ask.

He rubs his face. 'Alex, don't start.'

Start what? Alex's hackles are up. But it's not worth it. Aren't we glad she's not home?

'I don't really feel like cooking. How about we go out for Indian tonight?' he suggests.

'Can I go as… What I mean is, do you care what I wear?'

'Do you care what *I* wear?'

I hesitate. 'Why? What are you going to wear?'

He looks down at his work shirt. It's a bit crumpled, but it's all right.

Upstairs I wipe off most of my make-up, because I know it will make him happy. I still have long hair, but I could be a boy. I could be either. I change into jeans, a hooded T-shirt and sneakers.

We walk down to the Indian a few blocks away. We don't say anything on the way there. We just walk.

Inside we grab a table near the window. It's early. They've only just opened. One of the waiters is still making up the tables. Dad munches on a pappadum. And then he tells me about what happened at work.

'I had to do a quote at a chemical plant, so I arrive and it's all top security with guards at the gate and special keypads into every door. I met the guy I was supposed to see at the reception desk. These places are really quite vast so we walked a long way to his office. On the way he's telling me about his wife and kids, how he has little toddlers, and they're driving him nuts. He takes me into a little room and on the table there is a shoebox.'

The lady comes to take our order. I order a dal, and Dad gets a vegetable korma so we can share, which is awesome, because he's respecting me wanting to be vego. She hands me a soft drink and Dad a beer.

'A shoebox?' I prompt. I hunker down over the straw.

'Yes, and inside the shoebox there are all these little tiny cardboard pieces of furniture.'

'Like a diorama?'

'Exactly. "This is the room we need the quote for," he says to me. I told him that I needed to see the actual room, because it doesn't just matter what size the room is, but where it is, and whether gases or particles need to be exhausted, and the power supply, physical space for the unit, and so forth. Then he said he couldn't show me the room because it was top secret.'

'What do they make there?'

'Fabric softener,' he says.

'And that's a secret?'

'Apparently. Then I told him that I couldn't quote on the air conditioner unless I could see the actual room. I promised that I wouldn't tell anyone. So he rang his boss and they agreed that I could see the room, but I had to promise not to look. This guy took me down to the room and then he made me stand in the doorway, but I had to keep looking down the hall. I wasn't to look at the room directly – he wanted me to look at it with my peripheral vision.'

'Was he joking?'

'No joke. So I gave him a quote based on not quite looking at the room.'

'Do you think you will get the job?'

'I hope not! I don't know how we're going to get in there and install it without looking.'

I chuckled, not even because it was that funny, but because he's making conversation with me as if I was an adult, and there's no tension, we can talk about our day and have a meal together and relax. He's better when she's not around. This will be good. We can bach it for a while, Dad and I in the house together.

Our food arrives, and Dad dishes out the rice.

'I guess what I'm trying to say is that there are weirdos everywhere, and they can hold jobs, and have families, and be successful.'

Then he casts me a sidelong glance.

Did he just call us a weirdo? Alex asked. The spoon is in mid-air over the plate. Our eyes lock over the table. He totally did.

I shake my head. 'What the hell was that?'

'Alex, I'm trying to help you. I'm being supportive…' he starts, but you know what? I don't even care.

'Cht!' I say, like Cesar Millan.

I push back from the table and walk out.

'Alex!' he calls out. 'C'mon sport! I'm trying to find ways we can talk about it!'

33

YOU WANT TO know what the YouTube thing was that made my mother have an asthma attack and leave the country, don't you.

I'm just going to tell it really fast.

Ever since I started at Joey's I had a special note from my mother that I didn't have to get changed or shower with the other boys. I was supposed to use the staff toilet. Everyone was kind of curious about why that was. I wouldn't talk about it and the teachers got all panicky when the other kids would jack up about it. I don't know how much they were actually told, but I guess they figured out I was deformed all by themselves.

There was one kid who wouldn't let it go. Roger Bloody Sullivan. He had to know. He really thought he had a right to know why I used the staff toilet. He was so angry and indignant when no one would tell him. Seriously, it would have been easier to get changed with the other boys, and just wear a really long shirt or something.

After school one day, Roger Bloody Sullivan and two of

his mates herded me down to the laneway behind the old people's home, next to the stormwater drain. They held me down and tore off my school pants and undies, and then they threw them over the fence, into the drain. I had to climb over the fence naked from the waist down, and then scrabble down the concrete side into the drain to get my pants back, and I'm shoving my leg in and the stupid things were wet and inside out, and kept wrapping round my leg like a snake, and I'm trying hard not to cry, but I was anyway, I could feel the snot running over my lips, and one of them filmed the whole thing on his phone and then uploaded the clip on YouTube.

It goes for four minutes and fifteen seconds.

They are not even laughing. Sullivan says, 'Toldjuz,' at the beginning, and then all you can hear are cars going past on the bridge and the pathetic sound of me crying. They film me in silence and with disinterest, as if I am an exhibit in the zoo.

After that I stopped taking my medication, because it wasn't making me feel any better.

34

SO THAT'S WHY I left that school.

It's dusk now and I don't really know where to go so I just start walking. I pull my hoodie up over my head and shove my hands in my pockets. My phone beeps in my pocket, but I don't get it out. I keep walking.

It will be a text from my dad. He might be apologising, or maybe it will be another accusation of how I am hurting them just by existing. I don't want to know.

Yes, I have noticed how they keep telling me that I'm hurting them. It's obviously some kind of pact. But it doesn't occur to them to consider how they're hurting me.

The worst thing about tonight is that he waited until I'd let my guard down to jab me in the eye. I've got so used to bracing against whatever they're going to say next. I'm not just angry with him, but angry with myself for thinking that the conversation might not have barbs in it.

It hurts. It makes my heart feel racy and sore like after I did the hundred metres with Amina.

Our dad used to make us wrestle to 'man up'. I hated it.

He would pin me by the arms and it was terrifying, being trapped like that. I'd scream and buck, and try to knee him. I think secretly he got a kick out of hurting me, the way I couldn't stop myself from pushing those kids over in daycare. The only thing I could do back then was pinch him, and then he'd get all shitty. I enjoyed pinching him. The way he flinched away from it. I'd really get my nails in there.

See, we hated each other even way back then.

It's abuse, isn't it? I'm not being a pussy. But it's not the sort of abuse I could go to the Department of Children's Services about – my father wanting to wrestle with me, or my mother insisting that I eat French toast. I think that sort of thing would put me fairly low on their list.

You were there, you saw. They don't love me. They don't even like me. What scares me is that I've heard people who aren't loved can't love. Does this mean I can't love Amina? Is this why I am being so mean to Sierra? Are we always going to be alone, Alex and I? Maybe I'm a psychopath.

You're not a psychopath if you worry about being a psychopath, Alex informs me, as if he is the authority.

How do you know?

Because psychopaths don't worry about whether they are psychopaths. Psychopaths don't worry about what other people think of them.

Since when do you know so much about psychopaths?

Trust me, you're a freak, but you're not a psychopath.

I put one foot in front of the other on the footpath. I breathe in every four steps and out every other four. I wish I had my iPod. I imagine I'm listening to it. I walk to my own beat and sing under my breath.

I don't know what to do, or where to go. Do I go home? What for? I can't even go to a motel or something because I left my money at home. I don't have anywhere to go. The more I walk the further away from home I am getting. I will have to go there eventually.

A man walks past. 'Hi there, cutie pie,' he says in a voice that totally creeps me out, then he spins on his heel and ghosts me.

I ignore him. But I pull out my phone, as if I am answering it.

'Hello?' I say, and then I look at the oncoming traffic, as though I'm looking for a particular car. 'Yeah, pull over, I'll jump in.'

I stop abruptly, and he strolls away backwards, grabbing his crotch and gesturing. I stare intensely at the traffic. Once he is gone I check the stupid message, but it's not even from my dad. It's from Amina.

Hey you.

You know that expression about your heart skipping a beat? Mine does that.

Did she send that just now? Or did she send it the other day when I was feeling so bad? Do I answer? What's something smart I can say? My thumb hovers over the keypad. I don't know what to say to this girl. She makes me dumb.

S'up? I text.

I stand on the kerb, waiting, staring at the screen. Nothing. Argh! She's killing me! But I am smiling now. My heart hurts still. It hurts in a good way.

35

I SHUFFLE INSIDE the door, hoping to be able to get to my room undetected. My dad is standing in the hallway.

'Alex,' he begins.

I hold my hand up. 'Don't even speak to me! I don't want to hear it! You know, I'm tired…'

'Alex!' he says sharply, and there is something weird and desperate about his face.

'What do you want from me?' I shout back.

Sierra and Julia step out from the lounge room behind him. Sierra gives me a tiny wave. She is blushing. I'm going to throw up. I put my hand over my mouth, but it's ok.

'What are you doing here?' I blurt. I hope they stayed downstairs. All I can think about is the disgusting upturned plate of French toast outside my bedroom door that I step over twice a day, because actually, no, I don't think I should be the one who cleans it up.

Sierra and Julia look at each other. 'Maybe we should go,' Julia says with an arched eyebrow.

She thinks she has me pegged. She thinks I am rude and bratty, and that I'm embarrassed because I've been caught being rude and bratty to my dad who has played at being a nice man for the last however long they have been here.

This is the price I pay for being normal. It started with singing 'Roxanne' in class, but I didn't see it then. I have no excuse to behave badly in front of other people now. *You* know it's warranted, because you have all the information, but Julia will never know what I have to put up with. If I want Julia's respect, I have to rise above it. I have to be nicer – more gracious even than a normal person.

'No, no, no, I was just… How did you know where I live?'

'My mum. It's on your enrolment form,' Sierra explains.

That's kind of creepy, I tell Alex, but he doesn't care. He's taking it as further evidence that she has the hots for us. I don't really get why that makes him happy. I remember her telling me that her mother stalked her. It was one of the first things she said to me. And now she thinks it's OK to snoop into my documents.

'We were going to get our nails done and wondered if you wanted to come too, since it's just down the road,' she says. She's still flushed, and her eyes are bright.

Look at her face! She is so in love with me. 'With Amina?' I ask. Sierra frowns. 'No.' 'It's just she texted me before,' I say, indicating my pocket where the phone is. 'Just us,' Julia says. 'I can drive you,' my dad says. 'No, we can walk,' I reply quickly. We're all standing in the hallway and it's awkward.

Julia doesn't really want me to go and get my nails done with them. She wanted to see if I was telling the truth. 'Did you see the turret?' I ask her. 'Yeah, it's awesome. It's cold in here.' She rubs her arms. 'Shall we go? Nice to meet you, Mr Stringfellow.' Dad scrambles for his wallet and hands me a fifty. Outside, I shut the door. 'I'm sorry about before,' I say to Julia. 'My dad and I had a fight before, and I just needed some space.'

'What did you fight about?' Sierra asks.

'Oh, dumb stuff.' I wave my hand. 'He was being a bastard and I didn't appreciate it.'

'Like what?' she presses. 'You can tell us stuff like that.'

'Thanks. I'm over it,' I say.

'You didn't look very over it,' Julia observes.

I could make something up. Or I could actually tell them. It takes me a while to figure out what I want to say.

We walk along the street. I take long strides avoiding the cracks in the footpath, but I'm taller than them, and Sierra is almost running to keep up, so I slow down and wait for her to fall into step with me.

'He wants me to be different. He tries to accept me for who I am, but sometimes he slips and says things that make it really clear how much he wishes I was someone else entirely. It hurts my feelings, that's all.'

'What did he say?' Sierra asks.

'He was trying to be supportive. He said he knows of other weirdos who have normal lives.'

Julia gives me a look. It's ever so slightly softer. 'You're not weird. It's quite common really, isn't it? What you are.'

'I haven't met any,' I say grinning. We're crossing the street now, and heading through the car park, into the shopping centre.

Julia's eyes flick to Sierra and back again.

She's picked it like a nose, Alex says.

There's a nail place just inside the front door. I've never been inside. There are rows of tables. The nail artist sits on one side and the nail owner sits opposite. There seem to be a lot of implements under bright lights. The nail artists all have masks and gloves on. It looks like surgery. I wonder if it's going to be painful.

We get three places in a row. I surreptitiously consult the menu and pick the one that is twenty-five dollars. Apparently my hands are going to have a therapeutic exfoliation in botanicals. What the hell is that?

The girl cleans my nails. That doesn't hurt, but then she starts cutting bits of skin off around my nails, and then she scrubs them with a rock. WTF?

'Your hands are quite hairy,' my nail artist says. 'Would you like to wax them?'

'Um, how much is that?'

'Half-arm, twenty-five dollars.'

'Sure, why not?'

'I'll have that too,' says Julia.

The nail artist then rubs hot wax on my skin, lays a piece of fabric over the top and then pulls it off quickly. There's no 'this is going to hurt like a mofo,' no, just straight off. Bam!

I curse.

Loudly.

And all the North Shore ladies turn in their seats to glare at me. Julia starts to giggle, and then Sierra.

'This is insanity!' I hiss.

She tears off another strip and my eyes water. 'Goddamn!' I slap the table. Then I start to laugh too. Julia hoots. Sierra leans into me.

RRRip!

'Stop it, or I'm going to pee!' I screech.

36

WHEN I WAKE up I lie in bed for a while staring at the ceiling. I'm going to Crockett's today and I'm feeling great. Sore but great. I can still feel the burn on my arms, but I love the way they are silky smooth. My hair is getting a bit dready underneath where the extensions are coming loose, but I kind of like it. Like Avril Lavigne dragged backwards though a bush.

That's OK, I can twirl it into a big bun on the top of my head. I wear my cute butterfly T-shirt, some of my ugly old cargoes and stripy socks. You'll be able to see my belly button, but I have a nice flat stomach. I tie the sleeves of an old flannie around my waist – something for me to paint in.

After that I'm going to take my thousand dollars and go shopping. I want shoes with a peep toe and a giant, spiky heel. I want a short, sleeveless dress that flows from the waist down. I want a handbag – mint-green leather, all big straps and buckles that interweave with each other. Big enough to sling over my body. I want black wide-leg pants, and skinny jeans. I want a scarf that I can wear wrapped around my head and then in two long tresses down my back. I want some bright-coloured, chunky rings and bangles that will go *chingaling*.

My mobile is on the bedside table, I'm thinking who I'll invite to come with me. Julia and Sierra, but what about Amina? We could all go as a group, and then sit in the food court after, have a smoothie and talk about girl stuff. Or wander around window shopping, like we did last night.

I'm excited about the day ahead, and I'm also calmer than I have felt for ages.

I might even be happy. Alex must still be asleep. I wiggle my toes under my quilt cover, enjoying this moment where the day is full of things to look forward to instead of things to dread.

Like my mother.

Am I too hard on her?

I know teenagers are bratty and rude.

Is my mother the reasonable one? Because I genuinely believe that I am right and she is wrong. She seems so totally scattered to me.

The only way I can think to end this war with my mother is to give in, and say, 'Yes, you're right, I'm wrong, I am a boy after all, and yes, I will make myself eat French toast, even though I don't want it, just because you made it.'

Would that make her happy, or would she just find a new thing to get angry about?

When I look over these past few weeks, I can't see one thing I have done wrong. What's so bad that she needed to leave the country?

Argh! It's driving me crazy, and spoiling my good day!
Eventually I throw the covers back.

The upturned plate is gone from the doorway. I feel the carpet and it's damp. My dad is snoring in his room. He must have scrubbed the carpet while I was asleep.

The house is a bit of a mess. There are dishes piled in the sink.

After my cereal, I stack the dishwasher and put on a load of washing. I leave a note on the bench for my dad to hang it out and thank him for cleaning up the French toast.

I'm really glad because Mum and I would have fought to the death over that stupid toast, and now we don't have to.

Then I'm striding down the street in my steel-caps, with my bag slung over my shoulder, and my thousand dollars in my sock. It's going to be a great day. I skip for three steps.

I look in the windows of the shops in the little strip where Crockett's business is. There's a newsagent, a café and a bus stop. At the end is a second-hand bookshop. They have clothes out the front that smell like incense.

I can imagine Natalie and I sitting there, each reading a magazine, in companionable silence, and eating fruit toast. Like proper grown-ups. I hope she is a tour guide somewhere cool, like South America. We can decorate the flat with fabrics from Guatemala and Mayan pottery. I imagine her pretty and smart. We won't be besties, though. Sometimes we'll argue over whose turn it is to take the rubbish out. She will be like a big sister.

Crockett's almost doing a jig when he sees me, he's so agitated. He's pulled the curtain back from the window and the colour looks good in natural light. It's much fresher.

'What's up with you?' I ask, smiling.

'I have news!' He rubs his hands together, sitting on the edge of his desk. 'I did some searches, and your current birth certificate was applied for when you were six months old, but guess what? Before that you had a birth certificate that says you are a girl.'

It feels like someone has punched me. I'm getting pins and needles in my fingers, and I can hear a ringing sound in my ears. I'm pressing my lips together, but I can't feel them.

Crockett goes on. 'It was applied for when you were two weeks old, and then annulled when you were six months and replaced with the other one that identified you as male.' He stops. 'Alex, are you all right?'

'They knew,' I croak. 'They acted so surprised, but they've known this whole time. They *made* me a boy.'

Crockett nods. 'It looks that way.'

'What is wrong with them? There is something wrong with them. It's not just me.'

Crockett opens up his arms and I lean into him. He has a big furry woollen vest on.

'You were right, kiddo,' he says, patting my back. 'You know who you are.'

I cry for a bit, but then eventually I stop, and I'm exhausted. I lie on my belly on Crockett's carpet and he returns to his desk. He's tapping away on his keyboard.

It makes all my soul-searching this morning about my mother seem so raw. So naïve.

At any point in time between me being an infant and now

they could have said, 'Oh, by the way when you were born we thought you were a girl.'

The other night, for example, springs to mind. When I said that I felt like a girl, that was an opportunity to say that this was on the cards, rather than rolling on the floor and screaming, 'You're killing me, you little pervert.'

I ask, 'Can I divorce them? Like, can I be emancipated, or whatever it's called? Can I never see them again? That's what I want. I don't even want anything from the house. I never want to go there again. I want it to be as though we've never even met.'

37

www.motherhoodshared.com

I'm writing this from my overwater bure in Likuliku Lagoon. I've had a hot stone massage and three mojitos. I am feeling pretty relaxed. I haven't left the resort. I don't think I will. This place is perfectly serene. It's letting my mind slow down.

When I arrived I just sat on the front deck over the water. They bring cocktails and so much seafood. It was a little bit overcast, but still gorgeous and tropical. Then I put on my bathers and swam in the lagoon. The water was warm like a bath. I lay my head back in the water and floated. I could hear the water slapping against the wood pylons, my breathing and my heartbeat.

I am in another world.

I am also lonely. But that is nothing new.

What's wrong with us? We are three good people. We are all talking, but nobody is listening to the other. When I talk to Alex he is not even trying to hear what I am saying, he is so busy reading it for some kind of insult – some reason to be wounded.

Nothing gets through to him.

I want him to be happy more than anything. I want us all to be happy. I wanted to thank you all for hanging in there and listening, and telling me what you think. Even you, Vic! Lol! You make me think about things differently and I know you are in Alex's corner.

Please believe I am in his corner too.

She's my baby. She's so strong and fierce that I am afraid of her sometimes. But she's going to need to be fierce, because the path she is on is going to be so painful.

Heather

COMMENTS:

Vic wrote:

That's very gracious of you, Heather. It's easy from the outside looking in, but this is huge. It really is. I can see your heart is breaking for this little person you made. Bless you both.

Cheryl wrote:

Now you've both gone and made me cry!

38

CROCKETT SAYS I don't have to paint, but I do anyway. It gives me something to do. He spends the morning on the phone, finding me a temporary foster placement. He eventually finds a place for me. It's a lady on her own – not a family. It's only for a few days until they figure out what to do with me.

I want to ask him if I can move in upstairs, but he must have thought of that and dismissed it. If I ask and he says no, then I think I will cry, and he will be embarrassed and it will be really awkward.

Crockett thinks we need to go back to my house and at least collect my school things. He wants to talk to my father, and explain that I will be safe.

I don't want to go back there. I don't want to have that conversation. What's the point? What they've done to me is unforgivable. Ever. There's no discussion that's going to change that.

But apparently I have to have my parents' consent to emancipate myself. Isn't that crazy?

I take a really long time to clean the brushes, watching the water, burning orange, fade to clear under my fingers as I knead the bristles. Crockett leans against the door frame. 'It's time to go,' he says.

Crockett drives a van. It's column shift and it's full of crap – papers everywhere and what appear to be the ghosts of meals he's had in here. I push some of the debris over with my foot as I climb in.

He hands me some business cards. 'In case you need to ring me.'

'Ta,' I say.

'How do you think this is going to go?' he asks, rubbing his stubble as we stop at some traffic lights.

I don't really know what my father will do. I'm glad my mother is not home. Let my dad tell her. Maybe she will literally explode and then I can get on with my life.

'I'm scared,' I confess.

'Me too,' Crockett says, and I laugh.

We drive for a while in silence.

'I'm picking up Natalie from the airport later,' he tells me.

I imagine she is brunette, and fit, but small. Nuggetty. She might have dreads. She intersperses words of Spanish into the conversation. *Fuego!*

Crockett stops the car in front of our house. I am hiding behind him as he knocks on the door.

My dad answers and he looks perplexed when he sees me, then concerned.

Crockett shakes my father's hand. 'Alex has engaged me

as her solicitor.'

'Sorry, he, her what?'

'You might like to go and fetch your things now, Alex.' He steps back and steers me towards the door.

As I walked down the hallway I could hear Crockett speaking in lawyer behind me. 'Initially Alex engaged me in reference to some documents she wished to procure with which to process her enrolment – to wit, one birth certificate identifying her gender as female – but upon submitting applications, it became apparent that one such document had previously been rendered, and then annulled as of the fifth day of May 1998. As a consequence…' I'm not able to hear the rest of what he says as I head up the stairs, although I do hear my father curse.

What do you pack when you are leaving forever? I stand frozen in the middle of the room, because I've never lived anywhere else. I'm suddenly sure that it's the wrong thing to do. I should just suck it up for a few more years and save my money from my modelling jobs.

But then Crockett would have said, wouldn't he? When I asked if he could emancipate me, he didn't say, 'You should go home and work it out with your folks.' He didn't say that at all. He got on with the business of getting me the hell out of here. If he thought it was a bad idea, I'm sure he would have said. Wouldn't he?

Then I remember my mother throwing the French toast on the floor and blaming me, and hitting me with the phone over ordering the wrong pizza, and my dad saying I should be nicer to her, and calling me a weirdo. Strangers are going to treat me better than that. Especially if they don't know about the noodle. If I front up as a normal girl.

I grab my school bag and all my books. I shove my uniform in. My phone charger. The only clothes I'm interested in are still in a pile on my chair from where I sorted them the other day, so I shove them in a garbage bag.

There's nothing else I want from here. I stand there again for a minute, trying to remember everything exactly how it is today. One day I'll have to describe it to a therapist.

At the last minute I grab my pillow.

When I go back downstairs my dad is bawling his eyes out.

He's saying, 'Don't take my baby away,' over and over. He is clinging to Crockett's shirtsleeve.

Crockett looks terrible.

'I'm ready,' I say.

'Alex!' my dad calls out. His face is all twisted and red.

Crockett is shaking him off.

I get in the car and look out the window. My dad is kneeling on the footpath. He has his hands over his face. He is weeping. He looks as though he's praying.

'Oh God. Please! Please don't take my baby away.'

39

YOU KNOW WHAT it comes down to? Alex says to me. People who don't want to lose their babies shouldn't treat them like shit.

I asked Crockett to tell me more about Natalie while we drove.

He hoped that she would go to university. His wife wanted Natalie to do law. She seemed to enjoy being a tour guide. Crockett thought she would get tired of travel. He didn't think she was a people person. 'Doesn't suffer fools' was the expression he used, but she was very good at organising. She used to organise things when she was little. She used to get her brother's matchbox cars and make a car park.

I'm trying to fit that information in with my Spanish-talking dread girl.

The foster lady lives at the end of a dirt road. There's no public transport. She's going to have to drive me anywhere I want to go. I have a rehearsal for the fashion parade tomorrow afternoon. I'm not sure how I'm going to get back here. I suppose I could drop out.

We bump over a cattle grid, and wind down to her neat house with a wraparound veranda. I look through the window while we wait for her to answer the door. There's not much stuff, just wicker furniture, but no pictures or knick-knacks or papers anywhere. It's stark and a bit threadbare, like a holiday rental.

She invites us in, but she doesn't smile. Her name is Pam. She's got wiry hair, and grey podgy skin as though she's never seen a vegetable. Maybe she's nice on the inside.

She's not, though. After Crockett leaves, she shows me to my room. It's plain, but clean. It has a chenille bedspread. I think they stopped making them twenty years before I was born.

I unpack, and when I come out again she has made me tinned spaghetti on toast for a snack. That's nice, right?

'This is my first night away from home,' I tell her.

Pam turns the telly on.

'My mother is away at the moment. She doesn't know that I'm gone yet.'

Pam is flicking between the channels. She settles on *Grand Designs* with that snooty English man.

'But then she didn't tell us that she was going either. She went to Fiji.'

'Sometimes it's easier not to talk about it,' she says, not taking her eyes off the telly. Pam looks lumpy, as though she's made out of rubber. You could imagine her peeling her skin off and a whole new person climbing out from underneath.

Alex shivers.

The pantry door is partially open, and I can see row after

row of home-brand tinned spaghetti.

It wasn't a snack, it was dinner. But even that isn't why she's mean.

In the wardrobe in my room there is a stack of Sweet Valley High books. I lie down and read *Wrong Kind of Girl* from front to back.

It takes me ages to get to sleep, because this house is cold and has no soul. I'm wondering if I should get out another one of the Sweet Valley High books when I hear feet whispering across the floor and Pam's shadow falls across the covers. I lie really still. I'm afraid for a moment that she's going to do something unnatural to me. My whole body tenses.

Pam lays an extra blanket over me (that's nice), watches me for a moment and then she goes back to the kitchen, where she rings someone.

'Yeah, she turned up this afternoon. I don't know why I do this anymore.' There's a pause. 'Yeah, but the money's not *that* good, you know what I mean?'

I don't even know why this makes me cry into my pillow, because I don't really care what Podgy Pam thinks of me. Maybe it's because I want to go and live with Ned and Alice in Sweet Valley, and have a twin who is a beautiful cheerleader, instead of an imaginary wanker.

I get ready for school the next morning. There's no lock on the bathroom door, so I have a really quick shower, because I'm worried Pam will come in and see me. But I pause when I'm naked in front of the mirror, because there are breasts there. Just little mosquito bites, but definitely girl breasts. I dress quickly, and then I do the mineral make-up in layers with a brush, like at my photo shoot. I do my eyes all wide and manga, with pink eye shadow to cover the puffiness and the red.

When I come out of the bathroom, Pam is watching *Sunrise*. She turns, says to me, 'And you can wash all that off, for a start,' as if there had been another instruction before that one.

'It's OK, it's not against school rules.'

'I don't care about school rules, it's against Pam rules.'

I'm not sure how to politely say I don't care what she thinks so I go with, 'I'm sorry you feel that way.'

She narrows her eyes, and that's it. I can't believe how easy that was.

Pam drives me to the train station at about seven-thirty in her pyjamas. 'Have a nice day now,' she says.

It takes me another fifty minutes on the train. I walk into school as the bell sounds for roll call. Pam's place is not really very practical. Crockett did say it was only temporary. I wonder how long I will need to stay there. Could I rent my own place? And get a job modelling?

'You're late today,' Sierra says. She's been waiting for me by the glass double-doors. 'Did you sort things out with your dad?'

'Kind of.' We're pushing along the crowded corridor. Her arm brushes against mine.

'I thought I might drop by this arvo, so we can hang out. Maybe do our homework together or something?'

I fold my arms. 'I won't be there this afternoon. I'm staying at my Aunt Pam's for a bit.'

'Yeah, I went around to your house yesterday,' Sierra says, and her jaw juts out, as if she knows something. I wonder if she saw any of the shit with Crockett, or how soon after that happened she might have seen my dad. When he was still on the lawn? I have a vision of him kneeling there, and I feel bad for him.

'I met your mother,' Sierra says.

She's home then, I think, and I'm a bit panicked, because my mother will have a meltdown and I will cop it. Somehow. Her meltdowns have a half-life. I look at Sierra sharply, wondering if she's taking the piss. Wondering how much my mother might have told her already. It would be just like my mother to reveal all my secrets in some sob story about how awful I am to her. I can imagine her weeping, and really seriously thinking that she has a right to do that, and that everyone should be sorry for her.

It makes me so mad that my fists clench – it has nothing to do with her. Why does she have to make everything about her? Why couldn't she just stay in Fiji?

I hate her. I wish she would get run over by a tractor and lie there for days, and have to chew off her own arm. Then she'd have something to cry about.

'Good for you,' I say through gritted teeth.

Sierra stares at me. 'Have you got the shits or something?'

'What? No. Yes.' I sigh. 'I don't really want to talk about it now.'

Sierra stops in the corridor, and other students flow around her. 'What did *I* do?'

'Huh? Nothing!' I say.

'Why are you being so horrible to me?' she wails.

I frown at her, confused. 'Horrible? What are you talking about?' I shake my head. 'I'm not being horrible. I haven't even thought about you.'

Her mouth drops open and her cheeks turn crimson. 'You are so mean!'

WTF is her problem? Alex asks.

We're going to be late to class.

'Whatever, Sierra.'

This is how much I know about girls. I thought if Sierra was really upset, she would punch me in the face, and if she wasn't that upset, she would go away and cool down, and realise she was overreacting, and then next time I saw her we would carry on as if this conversation had never happened. I wait for her to punch me, but she doesn't, so I turn and head to science.

But when I get there, Julia is waiting with her phone in her hand and this thunderous face.

'What did you say to Sierra?'

'I didn't say anything!'

She tilts her head just a little. 'You do realise that she likes you, don't you? I mean, in that way.'

I shake my head, not really sure what to say.

Julia goes on. 'You should be grateful. She's not even a ... a you know.'

'But I don't like her in that way,' I say in a small voice. 'I just want to be her friend.'

'What about the lick?'

'The, oh, that. No, that was a joke, because Sierra said I was gross.'

'She doesn't think you're gross now.'

I don't answer, because I don't know what to say.

'You're not exactly spoiled for choice around here, are you?' Julia snaps. She still sits next to me, but she leans away from me, looking out the window and huffing.

After a minute or two, I turn to Julia. 'Look, I'm sorry. I don't really understand what has happened here. I was in a bad mood this morning, but that's because I have my own thing going on at the moment. I don't get why Sierra is upset, or why you are so mad with me.'

Julia glares at me. 'Well, if you don't get it, then obviously there is no point explaining it to you.'

40

HALFWAY THROUGH THE class I'm called to the front desk. I'm glad to be away from Julia's oppressive glowering.

There's a lady at reception waiting for me with her hand on her hip. I haven't seen her before. Her badge says 'deputy'. Sierra's mother is on the opposite side of the counter, stickybeaking. She has a funny look on her face.

'Alex Stringfellow?' the deputy asks, flipping through my file. She has her glasses on a chain around her neck. She doesn't put them on her face. She holds them up and looks through them, as if they were a magnifying glass.

'Yes,' Alex and I say.

'It has been explained to you a number of times that you cannot attend this school unless you are officially enrolled.'

'Yes, I've been meaning to —'

But she interrupts me. 'Without a completed enrolment, you should not even be on these grounds. We have no duty of care over you; you are not covered by our insurance. In short, you are a hazard.'

'I keep forgetting to —'

'That's not good enough, Alex. I have left a message at home for your mother to collect you. You will leave the premises now, and you will not return without the outstanding items for your enrolment, namely...' – she peers through her glasses at her notes – 'your birth certificate and vaccination schedule.'

'You rang my mother?' I whisper.

'You can wait in the foyer for her to arrive.'

I stand there.

'Well, go on then!' the deputy says, pointing to the vinyl seats under the honour boards. But a faint wave of concern, or perhaps suspicion crosses her face. I try to make my expression smooth like the Clinique girl.

Sierra's mother clears her throat. 'Sorry, I couldn't help overhearing, there's another matter.' Her eyes flick towards me. 'DoCS rang about Alex's placement.'

'Placement?' the deputy asks.

Sierra's mother looks at me. 'Your foster carer has returned your belongings to head office. She felt there was a personality clash and has asked for an alternative placement to be found for you.' She has that expression again, a twinkle – as though she is glad.

'Sour old bitch,' Alex says before I can stop him.

The two women exchange a look.

'I mean the foster lady,' I clarify.

'You're in care? Since when? I have no paperwork on this.' The deputy worries at the glasses chain around her neck. 'This complicates everything. I suppose it's too late to call Mrs Stringfellow and tell her not to come.'

Sierra's mother nods slowly. 'I would imagine so.'

The deputy slaps my file on the desk. 'If you had been properly enrolled, we would have received prior notice from DoCS about your status, and I wouldn't have called your mother.' There's silence for a moment. 'Do you want to tell me what's going on?'

'Not really.'

'It might help if I know.'

She tries to stare me down. It might work on other kids, but there is absolutely no way I'm going to tell her about the noodle.

'If it's a sexual thing, or a neglect or abuse thing, I need to know.' She rubs her eyes. 'Is there going to be a problem with your mother coming here? I mean legally? Is there an estrangement? Any restraining orders? Is it a custody matter?'

I look at my shoes.

'For God's sake child, spit it out. I'm going to find out in the end.'

But I say nothing.

'This is a mess!' She stalks back into her office.

The deputy is cranky, but not because she cares about me. She's cranky because there will be a truckload of paperwork to do, and she'll have to stay back, and she won't be able to curl up in the lounge and watch *Midsomer Murders* and down a bottle of Chardonnay. Boo hoo.

I wait in the foyer in the same seat Alex and I sat in on that first day. I send a text to Crockett:

Having trouble at school. Podgy Pam ditched me. They called my mother. She is coming here. She's going to go mental.

He doesn't answer. He probably doesn't even know how to text.

I don't have any friends. Only Alex. Isn't that pathetic?

I play Connect Four on my phone for ages. Every few seconds I look out the front door. There's a man up a ladder in the car park. He's changing the picture on the billboard. I can't see the whole thing yet, but it looks like it might be an ad for the fashion parade fundraiser, and I remember the thousand dollars, still in my sock.

Don't worry: it's a fresh sock.

Then my mother is there in the doorway. She is wringing her hands. Her face is all crumpled. It looks as if she has only put make-up on one eye. She's not holding it together. It looks like she's trying to smile but she looks like a crazy horror-movie clown. She's whispering something. She looks as if she is made up of pieces of five different women. She's going to come in here and blurt out everything. I can tell. If she does the rolling on the floor and wailing thing, I swear, I will take to her with my steel-caps.

So I close my eyes and do my fast clapping. I know it makes me look as if I'm autistic or something, but when I am clapping I am in my own space. Like meditating. That woman is not my mother. She's a liar, she's totally unpredictable and she seems absolutely intent on ruining everything that is important to me. Who does that to their own child? She's a crazy woman. I don't want her in my life anymore. We don't want her anywhere near us.

41

www.motherhoodshared.com

I came home from Fiji. I took a taxi from the airport, and David was inside the house. He looked wrung out like an old dishcloth. A lawyer came to the house today.

Crockett. This parasite has convinced Alex to sue for emancipation or something. Preying on a young kid like this. I can't believe it could be allowed.

DoCS took him away. Can you believe it? When you see those women at the supermarket smoking while they are pregnant and their little toddlers running around unattended in the car park, and they say *we're* not fit parents? When Alex has had his every whim from the beginning! There's not a single thing he could have asked for. I'm absolutely livid! Somebody is going to get a piece of my mind.

This is a mistake.

This is not my Alex. That lawyer has got in his ear and thinks he can make a case of it, well he picked the wrong lady, I can tell you that for nothing!

And then there was a knock at the door, and it was one of Alex's little school friends. Sierra. She wanted to see Alex, but I had the presence of mind to say that she was staying at her uncle's house.

She asked me the oddest question, she asked if Alex had a cousin who was a boy called Alex.

Heather

COMMENTS:

Susie wrote:

Be really careful. Be nice to everyone. Always be really calm. I still have supervised visits because I let my emotions get the better of me when my divorce first was going on. I left some stupid messages on my ex's mobile, which I didn't mean, and they are still being held over my head as a reason why I can't have custody of my kids. I was just angry and sad. I would never hurt my kids.

Vic wrote:

One step forward, two steps back. Sometimes you just want to reach through the computer and shake someone.

Susie wrote:

Shut yo face, axxhole. What do you even know about it?

Dee Dee wrote:

I don't think he meant you, Susie.

@Vic, this is a journey. We're humans. It's never going to be a straight progression from A to B. There's always going to be side steps.

42

THERE'S SOMETHING HAPPENING between my mother and Sierra's mother. My mother has gone pale. Suddenly she backs up. She's walking backwards, not looking where she's going. She abruptly turns right and heads out the front door. She looks like some kind of crazy remote-controlled doll.

I follow her, and watch from the doorway. She's stalking along, but she's not swinging her arms. She looks like a sleepwalker. The teacher on duty has seen her, but she is too far away, up near the canteen. The teacher starts walking towards my mother, slowly at first. Arms folded. Curious.

My mother is heading to where Amina, Julia and Sierra are sitting. She has a piece of paper in her hand. She's unfolding it. It flaps in the wind.

Oh no. I stand on tiptoes, and then I squat down, with my arms over my head. I don't want to know.

My mother stops. Sierra looks up. My mother is waving the paper in front of her. I can't hear what they're saying. Sierra sneers, backchatting.

But you can't backchat to my mother. She will explode.

My mother takes a step forward. She grabs Sierra by the hair. She is rubbing the paper on Sierra's face. She is screeching. I hate it when she does that. It fills me with dread. It makes my bladder feel weak. It undoes me.

Sierra claws at her face. She falls off the seat. My mother stands over her. Amina has her hands on her cheeks. Julia has shrunk against the wall.

The teacher is running now. Kids are crowding around, the way they do when there is a fight.

Sierra is scuttling backwards on her hands.

The teacher has reached my mother.

'Excuse me, ma'am,' she says in her penetrating teacher-voice. She takes my mother by the elbow. My mother is stomping her feet like a three-year-old. She's still waving the paper.

Another teacher – a man – is running across the playground. He takes my mother's other arm. They lead her away.

Sierra is crying. Julia puts her arms around Sierra's head, comforting her.

43

IT WENT KIND of crazy. I had to wait in the school counsellor's narrow, concrete-walled office, but I could hear my mother shouting in the foyer, 'I was just protecting my child!' and Sierra's mother going nuts, saying she had called the police, and my mother would go to jail for what she had done. But in the end they took my mother away in an ambulance, not a police car, after she did the rolling on the floor thing. They thought she was having some kind of fit. I would have told them that's just what she does when she's not getting her own way, but nobody asked me.

Sierra's mother took Sierra home too. Through the crack in the door I overheard other office staff saying that Sierra's mother would definitely sue the Department of Education, and she would probably win. She would go off on WorkCover, and be sitting pretty. They said it would be enough to pay out her mortgage, and then after a year or so she'd probably get a job in the private sector. Because whatever else anyone had to say about her, she was a good administrator.

I don't understand why the Department of Education

should pay for my mother being insane.

Once the ambulance has gone, the deputy and the counsellor come in and close the door. I want Crockett, but they call my father to pick me up.

I say, 'Look, you needed a birth certificate for my enrolment – now you have one. Do you want to ask my mother for a vaccination thingy, now that you've met her? Or are you happy to take my word for it?'

It doesn't matter anymore, though. I will have to start all over again at a new school. And this is going to happen every time, because I didn't just appear out of thin air. I was Alex Stringfellow who went to a boys' school. It's on my paperwork.

Unless I invent a whole new name, and get Crockett to say that I'm in witness protection or something, so they don't ask, but that will make them even more curious.

I don't see how I can get away from the old Alex. At least, not without a huge effort. He's hanging off me. He's quiet sometimes, but he's always there, like a shadow.

The deputy shakes her head. 'But I don't understand – you were previously enrolled in a boys' school?'

'My mother wants me to be a boy. She is, like, a total mental case. Can't you see that? That's why I want to be emancipated, and that's why I need to speak to my lawyer.'

The counsellor sits there with two pieces of paper.

'Can you explain how you come to have two birth certificates?'

I sigh. 'My parents had the girl one annulled and re-registered me as a boy.'

The deputy and the counsellor look at each other, perplexed. 'I don't understand how they could have done that,' the deputy says. 'I mean, why would the registry allow that? You can't just make someone a boy.'

The counsellor shrugs. They look at the papers again, heads together.

The counsellor has a coffee cup that says *World's Greatest Mum*.

I'm not drawing them a picture of the noodle. I shouldn't have to show everyone. I shouldn't have to explain myself to every person I meet.

'Who is the current legal guardian? The Pam woman has handed back the belongings to DoCS, so she's not the guardian. Did someone from DoCS call back?'

The counsellor scratches her head. 'I don't think so.'

I look out the window. They have a little rainforest garden out there between the buildings. A boy runs through to collect a tennis ball.

'Can we return her to the father?' The counsellor asks. 'I mean, is this a disclosure?'

The deputy is flipping through a big folder with 'Welfare Policy Manual' written on the spine. 'In all my years, I have never come across this situation.' She snaps the manual shut and slips it back on the shelf. 'What do you want us to do, Alex?'

I rub my eyes. I'm so tired. I'm going to have to go through this every time.

'I don't know. I want to be worrying about the normal things, like, whether I have a pimple.'

I feel the prickle of tears and take a breath. But we're not normal. Are we? We're never going to be normal. It was fun to play at being normal. Now it's time to get real. This is going to be as bad as what happened at Joey's. I could keep going from school to school, enrolling as a girl and seeing how long it takes for someone to find out. Is it worth it? Holding my breath like that? What for?

What other option do I have? I don't even think I can go back to being a boy now. I'm just going to be this endless in-between thing that everyone despises.

'Do you want to see your father?' the counsellor asks. She is rubbing her chin. I wonder what the right answer would be. I bite my lip. I do want to see him. I want to go home, but it's not home, really. It's a hollow place full of lies.

I pause and take a breath. 'I want to have a family who can love me as a girl, and just be normal. They say I am a weirdo and a pervert. If I was normal they would not be like this with me.'

The World's Greatest Mum says quietly, 'They shouldn't say that to you, but you know, you can't change other people. You can only change you.'

'Someone should tell that to my parents,' Alex says.

A lady from reception pokes her head around the door.

'The father is here,' she whispers, but when she pulls the door back it's not my father at all. It's Crockett.

He's all sweaty, because he hurried. He ran when he got my text. Crockett is my friend. He knows about the noodle and he is still my friend.

'Hello,' I say. My voice is all hoarse and wavery. I am so

pleased to see him that I burst into tears.

He sits down and he talks to them. He has his hands linked behind his head. Relaxed. They talk about literacy programmes, P & C meetings, the rugby programme and the recent problem they have had with plovers on the oval.

Eventually, I get it together, and then my father arrives.

His face goes all rigid when he sees Crockett, but they shake hands.

The deputy orders a pot of coffee.

Crockett nods at me. The most reassuring nod. It says Crockett's going to get it sorted. At least for now.

44

MY FATHER THINKS it's important that I go to see my mother in hospital. I don't really know how to get out of that.

We walk down the hallway, past people who have flowers and stuffed bears. I'm trying to figure out what to say to her, but I'm not coming up with anything. My heart is shards of ice.

In her room, she's lying on the bed, with the back tilted up, fully dressed on top of the covers. She's been watching television. There are Fantales wrappers all over the little wheelie table.

When she sees us, she chokes a little bit, and then she holds out her arms, as though she's expecting a hug. My dad leans in and embraces her, but I slouch against the wall with my arms folded.

'Alex, honey,' she says, 'come on over here.'

I don't budge.

'You're not going to be petulant, are you? I'm getting really quite tired of your hissy fits. If you're going to throw a tantrum, you should be throwing it at your little friend Sierra. Did you know she has been spying on us? She came to our house snooping, and asking if you had a cousin. She's the one you should be angry with – not me. I was on *your* side.'

Alex clenches his fist, but I deliberately unfurl it and press it against the cold wall.

'Come on now. It's time we moved past this, isn't it?' she says.

I nod.

'You can come back,' she says. She's smoothing a Fantale wrapper on the table with her fingers. 'But you need to understand that things are going to change. We have to communicate with each other. You can't go off and make your own decisions. We make decisions together, as a family. You're still a child, you know, however grown up you think you are.'

I rest my head against the wall and close my eyes. She's never going to change.

She goes on. 'You don't understand – this is about your hormones. It's like you're drunk. You can't make good decisions when you're like this. This is not a democracy, you know. And when you pay your own bills you can make the decisions. But until then you need to trust that we're doing the best for you.'

Trust? She's talking about trust? Alex fumes.

I remember the counsellor saying that you can't change other people. It might sound like something Oprah would say, but that doesn't mean it isn't true.

She's getting worked up. 'You've always had every single

thing you wished for. If you go out there on your own, you're just going to become a junkie, or worse! But it doesn't need to be like that. All we're asking for is a little bit of courtesy. It's not that hard.'

She takes a breath, and then she smiles at me. She has caramel stuck in her teeth. She has crazy eyes. She's a psycho. A psychopath is running my life.

I look at my dad. 'I'll wait in the hall.'

'Don't you turn your back on me, Miss Sunshine!' she calls out. 'We're having a conversation here! This is exactly what I'm talking about. Goddamn! Haven't you learned a single thing?'

We're going to have the same argument for the next thousand years.

It's better to let it go. And I've decided, that's it. Just like that.

It hurts, but it feels like there's a knot in my heart – it's just loosened and unfurled. Nothing can tie it back together again.

45

IN THE CAR on the way home I look out the window. 'I'm going to go and stay with a friend for a little while. It's my turn to have a holiday from you two,' I say.

'I want you to stay,' Dad says.

We drive in silence for a moment while I gather my thoughts.

'I think I could probably sort it out with you, but she deliberately went out of her way to humiliate and shame me in front of people that I care about. I don't think I can forgive that.'

'Your mother is having a mental breakdown,' he says.

'You know what she could have done?' I turn to him. 'Anything, except assault my friends in front of the whole school! And then she has the nerve to pull me up about *my* behaviour?'

'She's not well, Alex,' he says. 'When we love people then we forgive them and we support them when they're going through something.'

'Well, I guess I don't love her then.'

When I turn to him again he is crying.

This makes me even angrier.

'What the hell are *you* crying about? Who's supporting me through my thing? Has she been calling *you* a pervert? Has she been coming around and pushing around *your* friends?'

'I don't have any friends,' he counters.

'It's no wonder, because you're a —'

'That's enough!' he interrupts. 'Don't say things like that, Alex, it's hurtful,' he begins.

I swear under my breath.

'If you try to hurt people, then how does that make you different from what you claim your mother is doing? At least she's not doing it on purpose. Do you want to know why I don't have any friends? Because I go to work, and then I come home and parent you. You are now, and have always been, a hyperactive, self-obsessed little shit, and caring for you is exhausting. So, yes, you should cut her a break, because she's been doing it twenty-four/seven for fourteen years, and even a very strong person would be at the edge of their capacity, and Heather is *not* a strong person.'

He pulls into the driveway and presses the remote to open the garage.

'For the record, I always wanted to tell you about your intersex condition. But your mother was the one who was home with you. She was here. I wasn't. She felt it would be best to wait until you asked. And I should mention, you still haven't actually asked anything. You have guessed, and assumed, and accused.'

He glares at me.

'And when you're grown up enough to have a proper conversation, I am happy to answer any questions you might have.'

I'm lying on my bed. There is no pillow. I left it at the Podge Lodge. I'm staring at the ceiling. Yes, I'm feeling sorry for myself.

I don't really know what to do now. I want to ring Crockett, but I'm worried I'm starting to look a bit obsessed. It's just that I have no one else. I can hide here for a while, but I need to move out before my mother gets out of hospital. There has to be an end to this, and I can't organise that myself. Someone else has to find me a place. There's nothing to pack. The only things that I care about are in a plastic bag at the DoCS office.

Now I'm just waiting.

You could have a wank, Alex suggests.

Shut up, you idiot.

What? It will make you feel better. Endorphins.

My father is watching television downstairs. At least, the television is on, and he is down there. He's not usually home at this time. It's too early for him to cook dinner. There's not enough time to do anything else. This is where a proper dad would ask me to shoot hoops, or play Wii. I know he thinks he is busy parenting me right now, but that's not what I remember. I remember him holding me down.

And then I recall that some of the times he held me down, it might have been because I was having a bit of a tantrum.

You are a shit, Alex says. And it's not just Mum and Dad who think so. Those reports in the attic said you were a shit too.

I'm not sure what to do about my dad. We could arrange visits or something. He could take me places – like to the zoo or maybe we could go and see a movie. And he has to be nice to me, or I won't go.

That stuff about being grown up enough to ask was a cop out. Because that first night – back at the beginning – when I said I felt like a girl and my mother had the big hysterical fit, he left. He just walked out. That's not exactly grown up, is it.

My mobile rings, and I grab it. But I frown at the number. It's Lien. What does she want?

'Hello?'

'You're not at rehearsal,' she blurts.

'Didn't you hear what happened at school today?'

'Yes.' She waits, but I don't have anything to add, thinking it's self-explanatory.

'Are you injured? Are you sick?'

'No,' I snort.

'What's the hold-up?'

I just lie there, holding the phone like a nong, because I don't have an answer to that. I kind of assumed all of that was over now.

'You're our cover girl. You made a commitment to me, and I expect you to keep it. We've had all of the art printed. It's too late to change your mind. And, besides, I have a client here, right now, who is ready to sign contracts. I have vouched for you. I told her to bring her cheque book.'

Then Lien gives me this whole lecture about being punctual and professional, and how it's not a good look to get a reputation amongst clients for being a princess.

I'm lying there, grinning, because Lien is as mad as hell. She knows about the noodle, and she doesn't care. She cares because I am late. She cares enough about me being late to yell at me. But none of this is personal to her. It's business, and my noodle is irrelevant.

46

www.motherhoodshared.com

David brought Alex to see me this afternoon. You know that child did not speak one single word to me? She should be cranky with her little friend who did the spying.

But that's not what I wanted to write about. The thing is, they have admitted me as a psychiatric patient!

I tried to explain that I was fine, and they gave me this look as though I was, well, a mental patient!

I don't know what to do. I've tried telling them there's nothing wrong with me, but they're clinging to the thing that happened at the school this afternoon.

All I did was go out there and tell that Sierra girl that Alex had the proper paperwork. I tried to show it to her, but she wouldn't look at it. She gave me lip, I tried to make her look at it, that's all. If she'd just looked at it properly the first time then I wouldn't have needed to get a bit physical.

Fair enough, I lost my temper, which I shouldn't have done, but I am working on it. Under the circumstances, those people violating our privacy is a much bigger crime, I should think.

Heather

COMMENTS:

Dee Dee wrote:

Back up a minute, what exactly do you mean you got a bit physical? Are you saying you hit this girl?

Vic wrote:

Maybe some time out will do you good. It's an opportunity to reflect on what's happened over the last few weeks. You have been saying that you wanted a holiday from your life, and this is an opportunity to do that. And there's the added benefit of talking to a qualified counsellor who is going to give you some strategies for dealing with Alex. IMHO you should embrace this.

Dee Dee wrote:

Vic, you and I are in total agreement about this!

Susie wrote:

Don't tell them anything! They will take your kid from you! Just try to look normal.

47

DOWNSTAIRS I TELL Dad that I need to go to rehearsal. He mumbles something about having to go back to the hospital anyway, and asks if I can help him pack a bag for my mother.

He drags a suitcase out of the hall cupboard. It's a big suitcase, as if he expects her to be in there for a year.

I open the cupboard drawers, selecting things that might be useful for her, and stack them on the end of their bed. Three pairs of pyjamas. Some trackpants. A few T-shirts. My mother's walk-in wardrobe smells like her – that slightly sour tinge to her breath, and a little musty, like an old lady. It's not a fresh smell, or a clean smell. She smells unwell. She has for a long time.

It occurs to me that she might have a tumour or early onset dementia – some disease making her the way that she is. Would it make any difference to the way I feel?

If a husband bashes his wife because he has depression, does that make it OK? Alex asks.

I leave my father to pick out underwear, and go into the

en suite to get some toiletries.

She probably won't need much make-up, but I put in some mascara and a kohl pencil, some tinted moisturiser and a ChapStick – enough to make her feel made up if that's what she wants.

This is good – taking these things of hers and packing them in a bag, as if I am taking memories and packing them in the back of my mind.

I'm angry now, but maybe eventually I won't be. One day I will just be sad for her. It could be some time before I will even think of her fondly. I can't imagine that right now, but I can imagine imagining it.

48

WE PULL UP out the front of the school. My dad asks if I want him to come in with me. I would like him to, but I decide to go in by myself.

I'm sweating. I stand outside the door for a minute, taking deep breaths. Then I open the door. Everybody turns to look at me. I pull my shoulders back and walk in like a model. Not sexy, just long strides, as if I am going somewhere.

Lien is pleased to see me. 'My home girl is here,' she says. Somebody snorts.

I can see Amina now. She is looking straight at me. I can't tell what she's thinking. I don't know if we're still friends.

But Lien is leading me away now, to get dressed. There is a rack of clothes they have chosen for me. I will wait for Amina to come up to me. Julia is getting dressed. She's not looking at me.

They've made up a practice runway. It looks like trestle tables stacked together. Some of the other girls are walking up and down in their outfits.

When I get up there, they all move to the side.

I'm standing on the runway, and Lien is talking me up to her client.

Julia has this furious expression on her face. Finally she calls out to them, 'You know she's a dude, right?'

A few of the other girls giggle.

Amina shoots her a look.

I swallow, but I try to steel my face, because this is a job, and it could be a really good job. A ticket to freedom.

The door opens at the back of the room. My dad stands there, against the wall, watching.

Amina pauses. 'Sierra is really upset,' she says to me.

'Yeah, I guessed that.'

'But I understand why you wouldn't tell something like that,' she continues.

Lien calls out to me. 'Chop, chop, Miss Thing.'

I drag the next set of pants up my legs, and do them up under the skirt.

'I think you are courageous,' Amina whispers, and then she smiles at me.

It's just a little quiet smile, but it's the best smile in the world. It doesn't matter what anyone else thinks.

Afterwards I ask Dad to take me to the coffee shop near Crockett's office. I order some scones with jam, but when they come I can't eat them because my guts are twisted. I am picking them to pieces on the plate.

Dad has two cappuccinos in quick succession. He's looking at the wine list, and then he turns it upside down and puts the salt and pepper shakers on it, as if it needs to be held down or some hard liquor is going to jump up and order itself.

I squint up at the window that faces the street above Crockett's office. There's a little alcove where I can put a clothes rack and dry my smalls. I could plant some flowers in pots. Maybe hang a hammock.

'I have found a place to live,' I say.

Dad rubs his eyes with the heels of his hands. 'Alex, you have no idea. There are bills — responsibilities. You don't even have a driver's licence. How are you going to get power connected? You can't just decide to live somewhere.'

I interrupt. 'When I need your help I will ask for it.'

'You think we're just going to give you money when you ask for it? Alex, honey, you can't move out. It's not going to happen. Can we stop this? Please? Just come home. Your mum will come around. Trust me. This is just a rough patch. You should have seen her before the wedding. Granted, she gets hysterical. She doesn't cope well with change.'

I'm turning the scones into dust. 'See, you think I'm being a brat, and I think I am escaping an abusive relationship.'

I flick my eyes up to him and back down at my plate.

Dad's face is going red. He's going to start a rant but he stops himself. We sit in silence for a moment. He's jiggling his knee.

I'm twisting the jam pot around in my hands. 'You can still be in my family, but...'

His mouth drops open, so I talk really quickly, trying to get out what I need to say. 'Instead of always saying I'm wrong, or automatically telling me that I'm hurtful, or childish, or rude or whatever, you could try to actually help me.'

He throws his hands up. 'And now an ultimatum. Is that

what this is? We have to do it your way or else we can't be your *family*? This is you not being a brat?'

I have to concentrate on the plate and not look at him while I'm talking. 'It hasn't even got anything to do with you. You could, like, be constructive. Because what I'm saying is that I can't be with people who are trying as hard as they can to … to wreck my life.'

His face is red. His leg jiggles so hard that the table wobbles.

'Can you see that? How hard it is already? Without someone coming in and being' – I hold my fingers up like quotation marks – 'hysterical?'

He's considering it. He really is.

Remind him that he wanted this, Alex whispers in my ear.

'But I'm doing what you asked me to do,' I say. 'I'm talking. We're having proper grown up conversation.'

Dad sighs. 'I guess. But the conversations I have with you are never the ones I'm expecting to have. Every one is a friggin ambush.'

'Maybe you could think of them as a surprise party instead?'

His lip quivers. 'A surprise party.' He nods slowly. 'I can try.' He leans forward. 'In return you have to try not to see your mother as the enemy. Can you try?'

Can we try that? Alex asks me.

I don't think so, but Alex says that we can tell him that we can try.

We can definitely do that.

49

www.motherhoodshared.com

David has just been. He says that Alex is moving out! He says that they have started a dialogue. That's the word he used! It sounds more like Alex said jump and David asked how high, but I didn't say that, because he had this quiet sort of happiness about him.

David says that maybe it will be a good thing, because Alex will realise that he needs us. Except David said she. Definitely 'she' the whole time he was talking. I asked what if 'she' discovers that 'she' doesn't need us.

And he smiled and said, 'If you love something, set it free'.

So we're setting her free. That's the plan according to David. And I'm the crazy one!

Heather

COMMENTS:

Susie wrote:

I was thinking about that last post you wrote on how you got physical, and I wanted to say that it never did me any harm. Half the kids today have never even had any discipline and that's why it's all gone to hell.

50

LIVING WITH NATALIE is nothing like I pictured in my head. Not that I'm complaining, because it's a million times better than living with my parents, but I think I have seen too many episodes of *Friends*. A shared house is nothing like that.

I have a mattress on the floor in my room, and a bag of clothes in the corner, and that's about it. The room is so empty there's an echo. The first time I went grocery shopping I didn't know what to buy. I bought soap and other cleaning things, two-minute noodles and some hot chocolate, and even that was nearly fifty bucks.

Lien said she has work coming up for me, so that's good.

This evening I told Natalie I was going to order a pizza, and she looked at me and said, 'That's nice.' She went into her room and shut the door. She does that a lot. I guess she is used to living in hotel rooms.

Natalie has a television in there, and a laptop. I can hear it going. And she talks on her mobile phone. There's nothing in the lounge room. I went to the second-hand bookshop and bought all their Sweet Valley High books. They gave me ten for five dollars.

When the pizza came I knocked on the door to offer her some, but she looked surprised.

'Oh, no, sorry, I'm going to the pub with some friends.'

She does that a lot too. I don't think Natalie wants to be my friend. Secretly, I don't even think she wants me to be here.

Not much of a secret, Alex notes.

She's used to having this place to herself, but at least she's not telling me what to do.

I will work on her. I can be lovable. I'll show her my fast clapping. Who can resist that?

At school Ty has started calling me Lola, after that song by the Kinks. He thinks it's hilarious. I don't mind it. Lola's quite a nice name.

Ty still sits next to me in art metal. He doesn't hate me; he's just embarrassed for liking me in the first place. He still stares at me, but now it's all curious and confused, like a puppy with its head tilted. I think he will come around eventually.

He's helping me with my letter box, because I'm no good, and he is. It's going to be great. It will be a keepsake for this time in my life.

Sierra and Julia don't sit with us anymore. It's just me and Amina. We spend quite a lot of time down at the oval. I've been doing the timekeeping for the athletics team. It's a very serious business. All the runners have told me their best times, and the times they are hoping for. I love it when they finish running; they spin around and look up at me, because they want to know how they have done.

They're on the track together, but they're not racing each other at all, they've each got their own thing going on.

Today a boy that I'd never seen before slammed me into the wall when I was on the stairwell. 'Lola the molar,' he said. Which doesn't make any sense. I figured that he thinks my name is actually Lola, and the mol part is just a generic insult.

When he pushed me, I hit my head against the wall, and it hurt, but it won't kill me.

Another boy, who I also didn't know, shoved him in the chest.

'You're such a dick, don't you know she's a retard?' he said.

I laughed. It was a high-pitched, squeally kind of laugh so I can see how the second guy might have made the mistake.

I laughed because people are always going to give me a hard time. I might even get beaten up now and again.

But there are worse things than people you don't care about not liking you.

I laughed because out the front of this school is a giant billboard. It's me up there, arching my eyebrow, in a bowler hat, with the drawn-on moustache, blowing a kiss.

It's me up there, dressed like a girl dressed like a boy.

Also from **Curious Fox...**

Half My Facebook Friends are Ferrets

Fifteen-year-old Josh fantasises about becoming a death metal guitarist complete with tattoos, piercings and hoards of adoring fans. But it's not easy when his super-strict mum won't let him wear black t-shirts!

Luckily Josh has a way of coping with life's setbacks; it's only a diary, but it contains all Josh's hopes, dreams and frustrations (not to mention some great ideas for band names and lyrics!).

What Josh doesn't know is that his mother also once kept a diary, and a secret in there holds the key to Josh's life becoming a whole lot more metal.

Follow the fox at **www.curious-fox.com**

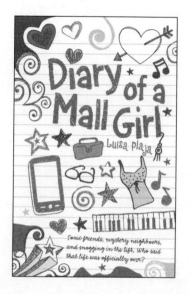

Diary of a Mall Girl

The mall is the heart of fifteen-year-old Molly's surburban town. Most teens hang around with friends there, get their first job there and experience their first kiss there. And Molly? She actually lives there, in the complex's residential wing.

But living in a massive shopping centre isn't as much fun as it sounds. That is, until mysterious twins Jewel and Jasper move into the flat upstairs. Suddenly life is a lot more exciting – and complicated. Will Molly get what she wants, or will it all come crashing down?

Find out the whole truth in Molly's private diary!

Follow the fox at **www.curious-fox.com**

Follow Grace Milton's adventures in the **WANTED** series.

WANTED: BOOK 1
GRACE AND THE GUILTLESS

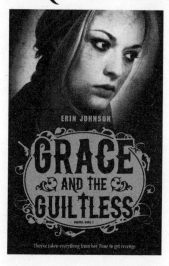

In one devastating night, Grace's peaceful life on a horse ranch outside Tombstone, Arizona is shattered.

Grace's family is brutally killed by the notorious Guiltless Gang leaving her the only survivor. Alone and desperate, she sets out into the wilderness on her trusted stallion, Bullet, with burning thoughts of revenge.

When she meets a young man called Joe, he takes her to an American Indian camp to heal her body and spirit. She begins to learn their ways and, despite her heartache, begins to fall for Joe.

Then she comes face to face with one of the Guiltless Gang, Doc Slaughter.

Follow the fox at **www.curious-fox.com**

WANTED: BOOK 2
GRACE ALONE

Can Grace make it on her own as a bounty hunter?

Leaving Joe behind has given Grace a new kind of heartache, adding to the loss of her family. She decides to become a bounty hunter, despite it being 'no life for a woman'. It will help her track down the Guiltless Gang, as well as paying the rent.

Her first test is a criminal known as the Black Coat, who's been preying on vulnerable women. She's about to put a dangerous plan into action when Joe comes into her life again, showing her what life could be like if she let go of revenge.

Then, as she struggles with her feelings, the Guiltless Gang appear tantalizingly close...

Follow the fox at **www.curious-fox.com**

NOTORIOUS GRACE

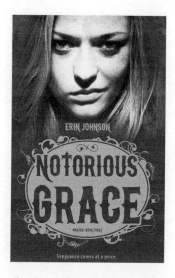

The desire for revenge will not stay buried.

Grace is slowly rebuilding her life: she's gaining a reputation as a bounty hunter and tentatively courting Joe. Then attractive fellow bounty hunter Kyle Black comes to town with shocking news: he's killed Guiltless Gang member Bloody Kit Doolan.

It's what Grace wanted, so why doesn't she feel like justice has been served?

Follow the fox at **www.curious-fox.com**

How do you live by the
rules if you don't know
what they are?

Amber

A teenage girl wakes up with no memory of who she is or
where she comes from. The only clues to her identity are
a dead mobile phone in her pocket and a beautiful amber
necklace around her neck.

Suddenly, 'Amber' has a brand-new life, a brand new name,
and a whole lot of questions. Disturbed by strange visions and
powers, she struggles to understand the rules that everyone
else seems to know.

How can Amber make sense of the person she seems to be?
Does she even want to be that person now? And by falling in
love with Dan, is she breaking the one rule that really matters?

Follow the fox at **www.curious-fox.com**

For more exciting books from brilliant
authors, follow the fox!
www.curious-fox.com